CHRISTMAS ON WAVERLY LANE

RACHEL HANNA

FOREWORD

A note from Rachel Hanna:

Christmas books are perfect any time of the year, right? As a Christmas Eve baby myself, I love this time of the year. Classic Christmas songs, the smell of pine and cinnamon, a really good hot chocolate, and the general feeling of happiness in the air.

Before you read this book, can I make a suggestion? As I sit here and edit my words, I'm listening to some amazing instrumental classic Christmas songs on Apple Music. If you have a way to do it, turn on your favorite Christmas songs, make your favorite drink, and settle in to celebrate Thanksgiving and Christmas with the whole Waverly Lane gang! No

matter what month it is when you read this, today
it's Christmas! 🌲

CHAPTER 1

"GRILLED CHICKEN OR STEAK?" Shelby cuddled up closer to Reed as they sat on her sofa, a movie paused on the TV in front of them.

"Why not both? I own a restaurant, Shelby," he said, laughing.

"I know, but having both just seems… excessive."

"Let's do both, honey. Some people may not like chicken. Or steak."

She looked up at him. "Who doesn't like either chicken or steak?"

Reed paused for a moment. "Vegans?"

Shelby laughed loudly. Reed made her laugh all the time. Sometimes, he didn't mean to. Everything about him made her heart swell. She never imagined love could be like this, and marrying him would be the happiest day of her life.

"You're a goof," Shelby said, playfully slapping his chest.

They'd spent a lazy Sunday curled up in each other's arms on the screened porch while the rain fell outside, hitting the tin roof above them. Those were her favorite kinds of days - where nothing had to be done, and they could enjoy each other's company.

So much had changed in the last year since getting engaged to the man of her dreams. Reed's restaurant had won Restaurant of the Year in Charleston, garnering national attention in a magazine. Business was up over thirty percent, and he was excited about that. He had even been contacted by a producer at HGTV interested in setting up a new reality show in the restaurant. Reed wasn't so sure about that idea.

Shelby still worked at the bookstore because it made her happy and filled her soul. And, of course, the book club was still in full swing. She'd grown to love those women, even Willadeene. Well, most of the time. She was Willadeene, after all.

"What about music?" Reed asked.

"How about an eighties punk rock band?"

"Don't tempt me. You know, I was in a punk band at one time."

Shelby turned and looked at him. "Really?"

"Yep. For about a week. Then my dad saw that I'd cut my hair into a mohawk with pink tips, and I got grounded for an entire summer."

Shelby laughed. "I need to see a picture of that."

He shook his head. "Trust me, nobody took a picture of that."

"In all seriousness, I think a DJ would be fine."

"You don't want a fancy band?"

"I don't think we're *those* people."

"DJ, it is."

"Are you excited about Thanksgiving?"

"Excited about everyone we know coming here to fill their faces with food? Of course."

Shelby smiled and looked back at the rain falling outside. "I think it's going to be lovely. I wish my mom could come, of course, but it's more important for her to get better. I hate that she'll watch my wedding on video, but at least she'll be here in some way."

Shelby's mom suffered from an autoimmune condition. Although she'd started a new medication three months ago and felt better most days, her doctor wanted her to minimize travel as much as possible for now.

"I wish my sister could come."

She reached over and squeezed his knee. "I know you do, honey." Reed had reconnected with his sister a little over a year ago, but she was traveling for her job during the holidays this year. She would be spending Christmas finalizing a hotel acquisition deal in Switzerland.

"Oh well," he said, pulling her closer. "The most important thing is I have the love of my life with me this holiday season, and there is no better gift than that."

"Ditto," she said, pressing her cheek to his chest as they watched the rain fall. Shelby couldn't think of a holiday season where she'd been more grateful. Life could always take a turn for the better, and that usually started with taking big chances and making big changes.

Moving to Charleston and starting a neighborhood book club had done so much more for her than she could've imagined. Her "family" consisted of people with no blood relation to her, but they held her heart just the same.

Book club days were her favorite. Shelby finished stirring the hot chocolate on her stove and turned it off. As long as everyone was on time, it would stay plenty hot enough. She poured mini marshmallows into a clear glass bowl and placed it on the kitchen island next to a smattering of mugs collected from various places she had traveled over the years. She supposed a professional would call her decor "eclectic," but Shelby loved to collect things that gave her joy. She didn't care if they matched all that well. They made her smile when she looked at them.

"Hello?" Lacy called out from the front foyer. She was always early. Nobody got there before Lacy. She made sure of it. It was funny, really, because Lacy was beautiful and always dressed to the nines. Most women like her would probably prefer to be a little late and make an entrance, but she was way too anal for that. She needed to be early to set up her food and help Shelby welcome everyone.

"Hey there!" Shelby said, wiping her damp hands on her apron. Her grandmother had taught her to wear an apron when working in the kitchen. Today, she wore a new one with little Christmas trees embroidered on it. She had purchased it from one of the many summer festivals she attended in the small towns around Charleston.

"I brought my famous apple pie," Lacy said, walking past her toward the kitchen. As usual, Lacy looked like she just stepped out of a magazine. Her white blonde hair was slicked back and pulled into a tight ponytail at the base of her head. She wore a pink cashmere sweater, perfectly fitted black slacks, and a simple string of pearls around her petite neck. If someone saw her in public, they would have no idea she wrote steamy romance novels. The thought always made Shelby smile.

"Can't wait to dig into that. Wedding planning is making me emotionally eat. I may not fit into my dress next month!"

Lacy giggled. "Wouldn't that be a hoot?"

Shelby's face fell serious. "Um, no. That would not be funny in the slightest."

"Sorry. I wouldn't wish that on anyone. I think you look great anyway. I'll be sure to watch you closely tonight. Only one piece of pie for you, my friend."

"Only one piece? Where's the fun in that?" Cami said, walking into the kitchen. "Where should I put the casserole?"

"Right over here," Shelby said, clearing a spot on the island. "Is that your cheesy chicken casserole?" she asked, leaning over and sniffing.

CHRISTMAS ON WAVERLY LANE

"Of course!" Shelby loved Cami's casseroles, and this one was her favorite. It was warm, gooey, and the perfect dish for a cool November evening.

Lacy pulled on Shelby's arm. "Imagine you're sliding into your wedding dress next month and, oh no! Your rear end causes the fabric to explode with a loud pop…"

Shelby slapped her on the arm playfully. "Point taken."

Lacy walked away, and Cami leaned into Shelby's ear. "Eat the casserole. I'll give you some yoga poses to stay nice and lean for your big day."

Shelby adored her friends. She loved her neighbors. She was grateful for her job, her fiancé, and the holiday feeling permeating the air right now. There was nothing like the holiday spirit surrounding her to put a smile on her face.

"What is that God-awful smell?"

Ah, Willadeene. The ender of all fun.

"There's no awful smell," Shelby said, rolling her eyes. "Cami made her cheesy chicken casserole. You like that."

Willadeene set a pitcher of sweet tea on the counter and leaned down to smell the casserole. "Maybe the cheese was bad. I wouldn't touch that with a ten-foot pole."

"The cheese wasn't bad!" Cami said, leaning over to smell the casserole. "Willadeene, you need to get your nose checked."

Willadeene grunted, shrugged her shoulders, and walked into the living room, plopping down onto the sofa with a thud. She made herself at home at Shelby's house. Actually, she made herself at home anywhere she went. Willadeene wasn't exactly shy.

"Sorry, I'm late, everybody." Joan came breezing into the kitchen, holding a bowl of fruit. She wasn't somebody who enjoyed cooking all that much, so she usually brought something simple. They hadn't seen her around a whole lot recently. Shelby had noticed it and texted her a few times just to make sure she was okay.

Since getting over her problem with hoarding and reconnecting with her son, Joan seemed like a totally different person. She also had a boyfriend that kept her busy, so Shelby tried not to interfere too much. She was happy to continue seeing her at the book club meetings and occasionally watering her flowers in her yard. Her boyfriend Randy helped her do all new landscaping, which looked beautiful.

"You're not late. We haven't even started yet," Shelby said, giving her a quick hug as she took the fruit bowl. "How are you doing these days? I feel like I never see you."

Joan smiled. "Well, Randy keeps me busy. What can I say?" Her face turned slightly red.

"It seems like things are getting pretty serious," Cami said, smiling as she squeezed Joan's arm.

"I guess you could say so. As serious as you can get at my age, anyway."

"You're younger than me!" Willadeene called out from the sofa. Shelby wasn't sure what the point of that comment was, so she just let it go.

"Well, I guess we're about ready to start," Shelby said, pointing to the living room. Everybody followed her in there. They did as they usually did at the beginning of every meeting—chatted about upcoming events or scheduling conflicts, and then they discussed which book they would be reading next.

After chatting about their current book, they went around the room updating each other on what was going on in their lives. Shelby talked a lot about wedding planning and how nervous she was to make sure that everything went off without a hitch.

"One thing I had always dreamed of was having a snowy wedding, but I don't think I'm going to get that here in Charleston," she said, laughing.

"Yeah, I don't like your odds of that," Lacy said, taking a sip of her wine.

"Well, it's going to be dreamy no matter what," Cami said, reaching over and patting Shelby on the knee. "You're marrying the man of your dreams and have such a beautiful venue in that old church."

"Yes, I can't wait to get married there," Shelby said. "It's going to be beautiful. I love weddings in old churches or other old buildings. So much history."

They continued chatting and then got around to Cami, who looked a little nervous.

"What's going on with you?" Shelby asked.

"Well, I have some exciting news. I'm going out on a limb, and I'm a little bit anxious about it."

"What kind of news?" Lacy asked.

"You all know I've been teaching yoga on the side down at the fitness center."

"Yes, of course. It's all you ever talk about," Willadeene said, waving her hand at Cami. Everybody ignored her and went back to listening.

"Anyway, I've decided to venture out on my own. I'm opening a yoga studio."

All of the women cheered for their friend. Even Willadeene said "yay" in an underwhelming tone, but at least it was something.

"That's wonderful. Congratulations," Joan said. "It's always good to make big changes in your life."

"You know that better than anyone," Cami said. "I hope it's going to be successful. I mean, I think we all know that new businesses fail pretty frequently. But I feel like I have to try."

"You do need to try," Shelby said, "and you'll do great. People love coming to your classes."

"Well, everybody except you," Cami said, poking Shelby in the arm.

"I've been to your classes, and I feel like I'm not physically capable of doing that ever again." Everybody laughed.

"I have something I'd like to discuss," Joan said. She, too, looked nervous.

"Why does everybody look like they're about to have a panic attack?" Willadeene asked. "You ladies always have these big dramatic announcements. Can't we have one book club where nothing is going on?"

"Apparently not," Joan said, "because my big news is that I'm leaving Waverly Lane."

The gasps in the room almost put out the fake fire in the fireplace.

"What? What do you mean?" Shelby asked.

"I feel like I need to be closer to my son and his

family, so I am selling my house and moving to be with him in Utah."

Everyone gasped.

"But you can't leave us. You can't do that," Lacy said.

"I'm sorry, ladies. I'm getting older and would like to spend my later years close to my family. But it doesn't mean I will stop being friends with all of you. I was hoping I could video chat into our book club meetings."

"Video chat? What in the heck is that?" Willadeene asked.

"I'll explain it later," Shelby said under her breath. She turned her attention back to Joan. "We will be so sorry to lose you, but I completely understand. You've got a whole new life ahead of you, and all we want is the best for you."

"What about Randy?" Cami asked, referring to Joan's boyfriend of a little less than a year. They were inseparable. Randy owned an antique store near Charleston, and they spent all of their free time traveling together, looking for antiques to sell.

"Well, I also need to share some other news…"

"You're pregnant?" Willadeene said, laughing loudly at her own joke.

"Anyway…" Shelby said. "Go ahead, Joan. What's your news?"

She smiled, her face turning red. "Randy proposed last weekend." She held up her hand, which she'd been hiding, to reveal a simple solitaire ring.

"Oh my goodness! That's so wonderful!" Lacy said, immediately running to look at the ring. Shelby was surprised she didn't pull a jeweler's loupe out of her pocket. "It's so unique."

"Thank you. He found it at an estate sale in Charleston. It's very old."

"Just like you and…"

"Willadeene! Shut your mouth! My goodness. Do you need me to pull a switch off the tree outside?" Lacy said. "Besides, you're older than Joan, so that joke didn't even make sense."

"It wasn't my best work," Willadeene said under her breath.

"Congratulations, Joan. I'm so happy for you and Randy," Shelby said, standing up and hugging her. Everyone else followed suit.

"When do you leave?" Lacy asked, sitting back down across from her.

"Well, there's lots to do before I can make the move.

I've already started packing up. We're going to get a place near Paul and his family. Probably something in a nice retirement community with a mountain view."

"That sounds lovely," Cami said.

"The area is just gorgeous. I can't wait to spend more time with my grandson, Andy. He's getting so big already. You know, ever since my Andrew died seven years ago, I've felt so adrift in my life. But now I have a fresh start. I want to make the most of it."

"Well, I hope it works out for you, but don't get your hopes up too high," Willadeene said before taking a bite of a dinner roll she'd snatched from the kitchen.

"You know, you should never get a job writing greeting cards," Lacy said, glaring at her.

Joan smiled. "It's okay, everyone. I know Willadeene means well, even if she doesn't realize it. Besides, nobody can dampen my excitement. I haven't felt this happy in so long."

"Well, I think this calls for a toast!" Lacy said, holding up her glass of sweet tea. "To Joan and all of her new adventures!"

Everyone held up their glasses, and Shelby smiled as she looked around at her diverse group of friends. They were all so different, but somehow they meshed well together.

"What about you, Lacy? Anything new going on in your world?" Shelby asked.

"I have something brewing," she said with a sly smile. "I'm not quite ready to reveal it yet, though."

"Oh, Lord. We don't need more secrets around here," Willadeene said, rolling her eyes.

"It's not really a secret, Willadeene. It just isn't finalized yet. What about you, Shelby? How's the wedding planning coming along?"

"You should know. You've helped me the whole way," she said, laughing. Like it or not - and sometimes she didn't - Lacy had stepped up to plan the wedding. She was often overbearing and opinionated, but Shelby had to admit she got things done. People listened to her. The vendors seemed downright scared of Lacy.

"I love our venue. In fact, we will take another walk around it this week."

"That old church is beautiful. I can't wait to see your pictures!" Cami said.

"Are we ever gonna eat?" Willadeene asked, exasperated.

Shelby rolled her eyes, as she commonly did when Willadeene was around. "Of course. Come on, ladies. We don't want Willadeene to waste away."

CHAPTER 2

SHELBY STEPPED out of Reed's car and inhaled deeply. The scent of salt air mingled with the earthy aroma of the wet leaves. There wasn't a time of year that she loved more than fall. The old church stood before them with its weathered stone facade, glowing softly in the late afternoon light. Sprawling oak trees framed the towering steeple, many of them with Spanish moss hanging from their limbs. She could tell it had witnessed countless weddings over the centuries, and soon, this place would witness hers.

Reed walked around the car and took her hand, his fingers warm. "Are you ready to make sure everything's perfect?" he asked, smiling.

She looked up at him, squeezing his hand. "I've

been ready since the day you proposed," she said, leaning in and giving him a quick kiss. Her heart swelled with gratitude—for finding Reed, a new home, a new job, and a whole new life. Her move to Charleston had been the best decision she'd ever made, and now she was standing in front of the place where she would marry this man—her soul-mate, the love of her life.

They walked up the stone path leading to the church entrance, and the heels of her boots clicked against the worn cobblestone. She wondered about the people who had walked this same path over the years—the couples, the children, the older people, all of those who had gone before her into this place. She looked up at the tall, arched doors, their dark, polished wood gleaming. Reed reached for the brass handle and pushed the door open with a creak.

The air inside was cool and still. There was a bit of a musty smell, which was to be expected in such an old building, and it held the kind of quiet that only ancient buildings seemed to hold. The vaulted ceilings stretched high above them, and sunlight filtered through the stained glass windows, casting patches of color across the worn pews.

"Wow," she whispered, taking in the grandeur.

"This place is even more beautiful than I remembered."

He smiled, placing his hand on the small of her back. "Our wedding is going to be perfect."

They walked down the center aisle, and Shelby couldn't help but imagine the day she'd walk this same path to marry Reed. She ran her fingers along the smooth, polished wood of the pews. When they reached the front, she could picture herself walking down the aisle with Reed waiting for her at the end, that loving smile on his face that always made her feel like the most important woman in the world.

An older woman with gray hair appeared from a side door with a clipboard in her hand. She wore a soft wool sweater and a warm smile that immediately put Shelby at ease.

"There you are! I was wondering when you two would arrive," she said, walking towards them.

"Hey, Judith," Shelby said, shaking her hand. "Sorry, we're a little late. Traffic and all. Thanks for meeting with us today. We just wanted to do one final check-in and make sure everything is set."

"Of course! Everything's coming along beautifully," Judith said. "I've been looking over the preparations myself, and I have to say, this will be a stunning event. Why don't we talk about seating arrangements?"

Judith led them toward the front of the church, where the pews had been temporarily marked with small tags indicating where family and guests would sit. Shelby looked around at the different markers, noticing close friends and other acquaintances. None of Reed's family would be in attendance at the wedding, which was unfortunate, but she tried not to bring it up. Of course, her mother couldn't come either, and she tried not to think about it. She wanted her there more than anything, but the drive from Tennessee would be too much on her in her condition. Reed promised he'd have someone use FaceTime to make sure she could watch live.

"We've spaced out the seating just as you requested. I just wanted to give you an idea of what it would look like," Judith said, motioning to the middle pews. "We'll add some floral arrangements here along the aisle for an extra pop of color. That's what your wedding planner, Lacy, suggested."

Shelby nodded. "That sounds perfect. What about the candles? I wanted to ensure they'll be lit just before the ceremony starts."

Judith looked through her clipboard and smiled. "Absolutely. The candles will be lit about ten minutes before the ceremony begins. This place will be glowing just like you envisioned."

Reed looked around, nodding his approval. "I think we're in good hands here, Shelby. This place already looks incredible. I can't imagine what it will look like when everything's ready."

She felt a wave of calm wash over her. Reed was right. Everything was falling into place for the event and in her life.

"I just want it to be perfect," she said, looking up at him.

Judith caught her eye and smiled. "It's going to be perfect. Every bride wants that, and you've chosen such a beautiful venue. We'll make sure every detail is taken care of, so you don't have to worry about a thing."

They spent the next half hour going over finer details—where the musicians could set up, how the guests would be ushered in, and the timing of the ceremony. Finally, they stepped back outside into the late autumn sun, which was casting a golden glow across the courtyard. Shelby felt lighter, the weight of wedding planning starting to lift off her shoulders.

Reed pulled her close, wrapping his arms around her. "Feeling better now?"

She nodded, resting her head on his chest. "I feel so much better. Judith is amazing, and everything is under control."

He kissed the top of her head. "I told you it would be. You've been stressing out about this for weeks, but everything will be exactly how you want it."

Shelby sighed. "I just want it to be special. This is a day I've dreamed about for so long."

"And it will be," he said, pulling back and looking at her. "No matter what happens, it's going to be our day. At the end of it, you'll be my wife, and that's all that really matters."

She smiled. "You're right. As long as we're together, that's what's important. Although…"

He raised an eyebrow. "What?"

"The one thing that I dreamed of that just can't happen here because of our location is a wedding in a snowy place. That's what I always envisioned in my mind."

"Well, it *is* Charleston," he said, laughing. "Not a snowflake in sight during the winter, typically."

She nodded. "I know. But Christmas is a time for miracles. Maybe Mother Nature will give me one."

They walked back toward the car, hand in hand, the old church standing tall behind them. As they drove away, Shelby glanced back one last time. Everything felt right. The venue was perfect, their plans were solid, and she had Reed by her side.

This wedding was going to be everything she had ever dreamed of.

Willadeene sat in her favorite overstuffed and very worn armchair. The soft hum of the television kept her company in the background. She wasn't even paying attention to the silly cooking show on the screen and wasn't in the mood for company today. It had just been one of those mornings. Her knees were aching, her hip was creaking, and her favorite tea kettle had gone missing inexplicably - because she had likely left it somewhere in the house. Ridiculous. Worst of all, the mailman was late again. She hated it when the mail was late. It threw off her entire routine.

Looking at the clock, she muttered to herself, "If that man doesn't show up in the next five minutes…"

A faint rumble from outside broke her grumbling. Through her sheer, white curtains, she saw the postal truck creeping down the road. Finally.

Willadeene pushed herself up from her chair

with a grunt, smoothing out the front of her pink and blue housecoat before she shuffled to the front door. She always liked to meet the mailman in case there was anything interesting or any news he had to share. After all, he got to see lots of things on his route. She'd had the same mailman for at least the last ten years. He was probably in his early 50s now, but he was aging quite well—one of those dashing, handsome men for whom gray around the temples looked good. He was married and had three kids, one in college.

Willadeene liked to find out everything she could about people. It kept her mind busy and sharp, or at least that's what she told herself. He never really had much gossip to share. He seemed like one of those people who thought gossiping was wrong. Maybe it was technically, but she liked to know what was happening in the world around her. He didn't seem to appreciate her colorful commentary on the state of the neighborhood, but he was always smiling and nodding, going along with whatever she said.

She wasn't stupid. She might be old and a little bit obnoxious, but she wasn't stupid. She saw when people were annoyed with her. She just didn't care.

Stepping outside, she squinted against the afternoon sun as she made her way to the mailbox at the end of her short driveway. The air was crisp today but not cold enough to warrant her wearing a sweater just yet. She had already changed from her summer clothes to her winter clothes in the closet, although winter in Charleston wasn't like winter in most places. She had some lightweight cardigans and a coat if it got too cold out.

The oak trees that lined Waverly Lane were starting to drop their leaves, painting the ground in a blanket of golden brown and orange. The typical hum of distant lawnmowers filled the air, but her mind was focused on the mailbox. She opened it with a quick flick of her wrist and looked inside. There were bills, a couple of flyers, and something else. A letter.

Willadeene was from a time when handwritten letters were the norm. She still loved getting cards this time of year. Of course, it was a bit early to get Christmas cards, and now that she was getting older, she knew fewer people. They died off, to be frank. That happened if you lived long enough—everybody around you started dying off, so she got fewer cards. But she certainly never got letters. She didn't have any family, after all. There was nobody to write to her.

This was a curious sight as she stared at it in her

hand. She frowned, pulled the small stack of mail out, and flipped through it quickly. Most of it was the same old nonsense, but that letter... well, it just stood out. Her eyes narrowed at the sight of the return address, scrawled in handwriting she hadn't seen in decades. She knew exactly who this was from. She could smell the perfume.

Gertie.

The name sent a cold shiver down her spine. For a minute, she just stood there frozen, staring at the envelope. She hadn't heard from Gertie in decades. After their falling out, she had made a point to cut her only sister out completely—her only sibling, her only real blood family. But she never talked about her. She never even considered her anymore. She didn't think of her as family. They hadn't spoken in over thirty years. That woman had caused her nothing but trouble—constantly stirring things up, making Willadeene's life a mess with her selfish antics.

She turned the letter over in her hands, looking at it like a bomb that might explode. The envelope was plain, nothing special, but that handwriting— she would have known it anywhere. Slanted, slightly messy, loops too large for anyone's liking, and she had topped it off with a stamp that had red roses on it—Willadeene's least favorite flower.

Willadeene muttered under her breath, shaking her head. "What could she possibly want now?"

She wanted to tear that letter up right then and there, just rip it to shreds and scatter it in the wind. But instead, her fingers trembled a bit as she slid her thumb under the flap, carefully breaking the seal. Why she hadn't just tossed it in the trash can, she wasn't sure. But here she was, standing in her driveway, wearing her housecoat, opening the first letter she had received from her sister in over three decades.

The paper was folded neatly inside, and Willadeene could still see that familiar handwriting. It looked slightly shakier. Her heart lurched in her chest—a sensation she tried to ignore.

"It's too late, Gertie," she muttered to herself, "far too late for this."

Instead of tossing the letter on the ground, Willadeene started to read. Her eyes scanned the words quickly. Whatever Gertie had to say, Willadeene knew it was nothing good—probably some lame attempt at reconciling, asking for forgiveness, or looking for help. The woman always had a knack for showing up when she needed something.

As the words sank in, Willadeene's face hardened. She scoffed loudly, curling her lip in disdain. The nerve of Gertie, writing after all this time. Did she think a bunch of words on paper would fix decades of damage? Did she really think Willadeene would just forget everything that had happened?

She shook her head again, crumpling the letter in her fist. "Not a chance," she hissed to herself, stuffing the letter into the pocket of her housecoat. Gertie had made her bed years ago, and Willadeene wouldn't let her just come strolling back into her life like nothing had ever happened.

She turned to go back inside, something stirring deep within her—emotions she wasn't ready to acknowledge. Despite her outward disdain, that letter had unsettled her in a way she didn't expect. There was a part of her, buried beneath layers of stubbornness and pride, that felt uneasy. She didn't trust Gertie. She never had, and the fact that her sister had reached out at all gnawed at her. What did she really want? And why now? And why did Willadeene feel herself caring?

These questions continued simmering in the back

of her mind as she walked up the driveway and into the house. Gertie's words meant nothing, she told herself. Willadeene had built a life without her. She didn't need her sister coming to invade her peace— not after all these years. Peace might have been too big of a word. Willadeene didn't feel all that peaceful most of the time, but she had plenty to keep her busy. Her book club, her garden, her nosy habits around the neighborhood—that was enough of a life. It had to be.

She stepped back into her house, feeling as though something had shifted inside her. That letter felt like it weighed heavily as if a large rock was in her pocket. It was now an unwanted reminder of her past. She sat back down in her chair, pulled the letter out again, and smoothed it across her lap. She stared at it for a long time before folding it up tighter this time and shoving it into the drawer of her side table. Out of sight, out of mind.

Lacy sat at her kitchen table, tapping her pen against her favorite notebook. The freshly brewed coffee scent swirled in the air around the kitchen, but she was already giddy with excitement from her latest idea. She had always loved getting lost in stories she created under her pen name, Jasmine Cain. It was her escape and her joy—crafting these tales of passion and heartbreak with happy endings. Being a romance novelist wasn't just her job. It was one of the things that filled her soul, along with her children, of course.

Her phone buzzed suddenly, startling her as it vibrated across the table. She looked down and saw her agent's name, Emily, flashing on the screen. Emily rarely called out of the blue unless it was something really big. Lacy immediately grabbed the phone and put it on speaker.

"Hey, Em, what's going on?"

"Lacy, you're not going to believe this," Emily said, her voice full of excitement. Emily was one of those people who had given her a chance when she first started writing, and now they had both ridden Jasmine Cain's success all the way to the bank.

Lacy's pulse quickened. "What is it?"

"Well, you remember how I told you I was putting out some feelers for some of your books to see if we could get any TV or film interest? I just got off the phone with a producer. They've read your *Southern Flames* series, and get this—they want to turn it into a movie or maybe even a series for a major streaming service."

Lacy froze, the pen dangling in her hand. "Wait, what? A movie? For my books?"

"Yes!" Emily said, practically squealing. "Apparently, one of the producers took your first book on vacation, and she was so hooked that she read the whole series in a week. She thinks it has great potential for an adaptation."

Lacy's mind raced. She had always dreamed of her books reaching more people, but a movie or a series? That was beyond anything she had allowed herself to imagine. "I don't even know what to say."

"Well, you don't have to say much for right now. They're just starting to talk about it, but I wanted to give you the heads-up because they seem very enthusiastic. The streaming service they're thinking about using is also going to work together with them for a proposal to see about optioning the rights."

Lacy leaned back in her chair, feeling her heart thud against her chest. "This is unreal. I mean, I love writing my books, but I never thought something like this could happen to me. Do you think this could really go through?"

"It's very early days, but the buzz is good, Lacy. Really good. It seems like they would want to jump on it quickly because of the popular trends right now. I know you love your characters, and from what I've heard, these producers are committed to staying true to the heart of the stories. You've built this world that people can't resist."

Lacy grinned. The world she had created as Jasmine Cain had always felt real to her, but the idea of seeing it come to life on a screen? Well, that was something else entirely.

"So what now?" she asked, trying to remain calm. Her kids were napping downstairs, and she definitely didn't need to jump up and scare them to death.

"Well, we wait for the formal proposal and see what the producers come back with. In the meantime, keep this quiet. We don't want to jinx anything before the ink is dry."

"Got it," Lacy said, biting her lip. How would she ever keep from telling her friends this? "This is amazing. A movie or a series, I can't even wrap my head around it."

"I know, it's huge. I've been pushing for this, and I think it might finally happen. These producers are serious, Lacy."

They chatted for a few more minutes before hanging up the phone. Lacy sat there in stunned silence, a smile seemingly permanently plastered on her face. This could be something big. Those words echoed in her head. She pictured her characters coming to life on a screen. Which actors or actresses would she want to play the parts?

She clutched the notebook she'd been scribbling in earlier, realizing just how far she'd come from being a stay-at-home mom, unhappy in her marriage, to a successful romance novelist. Writing had always been her passion, and now there was a chance her passion would leap right off the page and onto the screen.

CHAPTER 3

SHELBY STOOD IN THE KITCHEN, stirring the giant bowl of mashed potatoes to which she'd added butter and roasted garlic. She swirled in the last bit of butter. The turkey was in the oven, the stuffing was warming, and several side dishes lined the countertops and the bar. She could hear laughter drifting in from the living room, where her friends had gathered to chat before Thanksgiving dinner. The warmth of everything—the familiar sounds of friendship, the scent of Thanksgiving dinner in the air—filled her heart with so much gratitude that she worried it might just burst.

This Thanksgiving was different. It was unique. It wasn't just about her upcoming wedding but the sense of change that had happened in her life and the lives of her friends. Joan would be moving after the holiday season, and though she was trying not to dwell on that thought, today felt like the beginning of the end for their little Waverly Lane family. She just wanted everything to be perfect, even though her mind was racing with thoughts of her wedding, decorating for Christmas, doing charity work, and even working at the bookstore.

Shelby looked into the living room as she wiped her hands on her apron. Lacy was sitting on the edge of the sofa, her usual composed self, but something seemed slightly different tonight. She wore a beautiful red button-up cardigan with jeweled buttons, black slacks, and shiny black pumps. Her hair was in its typical pulled-back style, with a bun at the base of her head, but Shelby noticed that Lacy's fingers were drumming absentmindedly on her knee like she was holding on to something—some big news. There always seemed to be some big news going on in their group.

Willadeene, predictably, had taken the prime spot on the sofa, her arms crossed and a slightly distant expression on her face. She seemed a little bit off tonight, quieter than usual. That was a blessing, given that Willadeene was rarely quiet, but Shelby made a mental note to check in with her later. She might be difficult, but Shelby could tell something was bothering her. Like it or not, she was a part of their group, part of their dysfunctional little neighborhood family.

"Shelby, do you need any help in there?" a voice floated through the air of the kitchen and pulled Shelby out of her daydream. A moment later, Joan appeared in the doorway, a warm and comforting smile on her face, as always.

"I think I've got it under control, but you know me—I'm always open to help," Shelby said, laughing. She gestured to the counter, where all the dishes were lined up.

Joan laughed, pushing up the sleeves of her blouse. "Good. I'll carve the turkey. That'll make me good for something. You've got enough on your plate."

Shelby smiled gratefully. Joan always had a way of making things easier, and Shelby couldn't help but feel a pang of sadness, thinking this would be their last big event together before Joan moved to be closer to her son.

She walked over and turned off the oven, removing the turkey and setting it on the counter.

"How's everything going, honey? You must be buried in wedding planning," Joan said, taking the carving knife from the block and walking toward the turkey.

"Oh, don't remind me," Shelby said, groaning playfully. "It's going fine, of course. Lacy's doing a great job planning, and Reed is the easiest fiancé to ever walk the earth, but I still have a hundred little things to do. Reed keeps telling me everything will be okay, but I can't help feeling like I'm forgetting something or I'm going to mess something up."

Joan grinned. "That's what weddings are for, darling—the joy of feeling completely over-whelmed."

Shelby laughed as Joan began carving the turkey. "I guess that's one way to look at it. I should be thankful for the chaos because I have built a beau-tiful life here."

From the living room, Shelby heard Lacy's voice rise above the others, her tone light but with a hint of something bubbling under the surface. Shelby leaned closer to the doorway, trying to listen and see if she could hear what was happening.

"What about you, Lacy?" Cami asked. "You sure have been quiet tonight."

Lacy waved a hand dismissively as Shelby watched the scene from the kitchen doorway. "Oh, I'm just keeping busy," she said uncomfortably.

Shelby raised an eyebrow. *That's an understatement*, she thought. Lacy loved her books, and Shelby had a sneaking suspicion that something was going on that was bigger than what she was telling everyone, but maybe Lacy just wasn't ready to share. Hopefully, everything was okay with her and her children. She had taken on a lot to help Shelby plan the wedding, and she was a very busy author on top of it, but there was something about Lacy tonight— she was practically glowing.

"Come on," Cami pressed, her smile mischievous. "You're not fooling anybody. What's going on? You're always the first one to throw out the gossip."

Lacy opened her mouth and then closed it quickly, shaking her head with a slight giggle. "I'll tell you when the time is right." She pressed her lips together to keep from saying whatever it was.

Cami and Joan exchanged glances from across the room, but everybody let it go for now, turning the conversation back to the upcoming charity event for the foster children in the area. Shelby and Joan walked out of the kitchen and into the living room.

"I think this year is going to be our best yet," Joan said. "We've raised so much more money than last year, and the kids are going to be thrilled with all the gifts we're going to be able to buy for them."

Shelby's heart warmed. The women participated in this event every year, but this year felt different, maybe because it would be Joan's last before she moved.

"I was thinking," Shelby said, walking further into the living room and addressing Willadeene directly. She was still sitting there with her arms crossed. "Would you like to come with me next week, Willadeene, when I go Christmas shopping for the foster kids?"

Willadeene blinked, clearly caught off guard. "Me? Christmas shopping? With my hip?"

"Yes," Shelby said. "I thought maybe it might be nice—get you out of the house, grab lunch, pick out some great gifts. You don't have a whole lot on your schedule these days. I figured you might think it was fun to go out."

Willadeene huffed a bit, shifting in her seat. "I guess I could go if only to make sure you don't pick out anything ridiculous for those poor kids. They don't need silly toys with all the lights and sounds. That stuff is nonsense—cheap plastic."

Shelby bit her lip to stop herself from laughing. "Don't worry, Willadeene. I'll let you oversee the toy selection."

Joan caught Shelby's eye, her smile soft as she

mouthed, *"That's sweet of you."* Shelby shrugged. She knew Willadeene didn't have much going on—no family, no friends other than them—and despite her prickly personality, Shelby did feel a little sorry for her, especially at this time of year.

By the time dinner was served, the conversation had turned to Shelby's wedding again, as it often did. Lacy seemed to finally relax. The group settled around the long table, filling their plates with turkey, stuffing, and all the fixings—homemade cranberry sauce, salad, yeast rolls, and a giant pitcher of sweet tea, of course.

"So," Cami said, looking over at Shelby, "have you had the final dress fitting? Do you think you're gonna survive all this planning?"

Shelby tucked a stray hair behind her ear as Reed smiled at her from across the table. "Barely. It's amazing how many little details there are. The first time I got married, we didn't have a big wedding like this."

"You've got this, Shelby. Everything's going to be perfect," Reed said for the hundredth time.

Lacy raised her glass of tea. "To Shelby and her soon-to-be perfect wedding. Oh, and her handsome groom, I suppose."

Everybody laughed and raised their glasses.

Shelby blushed, feeling love from all corners of the room.

As the night wore on and the plates were cleared away, she felt a sense of peace wash over her. She loved listening to everybody's conversations— talking about Joan's move, wondering about Lacy's mysterious news, and observing Willadeene's odd behavior.

After dessert, which was, of course, pumpkin pie with whipped cream, Shelby looked at the towering box she had dragged into the foyer earlier in the day —her fake Christmas tree, waiting to be assembled.

"I still don't understand why you don't get a real tree," Willadeene said, standing in the foyer, staring at the large box.

"I told you this last year, Willadeene—I'm allergic."

"Who on earth is allergic to a tree?"

"Millions of people around the world," Cami said, rolling her eyes.

"I have an idea," Shelby said, turning to all of them. "Since you're all here and I need help, why don't we put up this Christmas tree?"

Cami's eyes widened. "That thing is huge, isn't it?"

"Only twelve feet," Shelby said with a grin. "I need all hands on deck."

"Count me in," Joan said, standing and pushing up her sleeves again. "I'll take any excuse to start decorating early."

"Me too," Lacy said, walking toward the box. "Let's get this holiday season started."

As they worked together to assemble the tree, there was laughter, good-natured grumbling from Cami about the number of ornaments Shelby owned, and plenty of commentary from Willadeene, who remained firmly seated on the couch. She said she was "directing."

"You're putting that ornament in the wrong place," she called out as Joan reached for a branch.

"Thanks for the advice, Willadeene," Joan said in a monotone voice.

Standing back and observing, Reed jumped in to help Shelby string the lights. And before long, a twelve-foot tree stood proudly in the foyer, twinkling with multicolored lights and adorned with what seemed to be hundreds of ornaments. Reed walked up the stairs next to the tree and put the star on top, completing the look.

Shelby stood back with her hands on her hips,

admiring their handiwork. "It's perfect," she said softly.

As her friends gathered around, Shelby couldn't help but think this was the beginning of a new chapter. The holiday season had officially begun, and with it, the countdown to her wedding and all the changes that would follow—building a family and learning to be a wife. She could see some melancholy in Joan's eyes, so she walked over and put her arm around her.

She was going to miss having Joan right here on Waverly Lane, but for now, there was nothing but warmth and laughter in the glow of the Christmas tree, her life filled with love and friendship she never knew was possible.

Cami stood in the center of her new yoga studio space, looking around with a mixture of anxiety and excitement. The room was filled with natural light from the large windows that lined one whole wall, facing the sidewalk outside. Off in the distance, she could see the Charleston Bridge and a multitude of live oak trees with Spanish moss hanging from them. She truly loved where she lived in the South

Carolina Lowcountry. The light through the windows cast a warm glow on the gleaming hardwood floors. The walls were still a stark and empty white color. That's why she and Shelby were here today. They would paint them a soothing green, a color Cami hoped would bring peace and tranquility to everyone while also bringing the outdoors inside.

She held a paint roller in one hand, ready to transform her space. But the weight of all of this responsibility was hitting her. This wasn't some small project. This was her new business, her future. She was responsible for everything. The bills, teaching the classes, and managing any staff she hired. It was more than she had ever taken on in her life. And as much as she tried to focus just on the excitement, she felt this gnawing fear in the pit of her stomach.

"I don't know, Shelby," she said, breaking the silence as she dipped her roller into the pale green paint. "This feels like such a huge deal. I mean, what if nobody shows up for classes? What if I fail? I'll be the laughingstock of town."

Shelby was standing on the other side of the room with her own roller in hand. She smiled. "You're not going to fail, Cami. You're a strong, independent, business-minded woman. You're going to be amazing. Trust me."

Cami sighed and pushed the roller against the wall, watching the green paint spread across the surface and envelop the white, boring walls. "But what if I'm not amazing? What if I'm just okay, you know, like average? I'm not sure I can handle being responsible for everything. Scheduling the classes, teaching the classes, rent, marketing, keeping this place clean. It's all on me now. If something goes wrong, there's nobody else to fix it, nobody else to blame."

Shelby moved closer, working the paint along the wall in smooth, long strokes. "I know it feels over-whelming right now. I've been there. I ran my own real estate business for years. But you're passionate about yoga. You've been teaching for a long time. People already love your classes. You have a waiting list, for goodness' sake. This space is just the next step. It's yours. You're going to create something beautiful here."

Cami paused, her roller suspended in midair. "What if I'm not a good businesswoman? Maybe I'm just a good yoga teacher, but that doesn't mean I'm equipped to run a whole business. I've always taught somewhere else, where other people were responsible for all those things I mentioned. Working under somebody else's roof. Now it's all on me."

Shelby stopped what she was doing and leaned her roller against the wall, turning to face Cami. "I understand how you're feeling. When I left my real estate business, I had no idea what I would do with my life. I was scared out of my mind. It was all I had ever known. There was no safety net. But I knew I had to take a leap of faith because staying in that career or even in my bad marriage that didn't make me happy was worse than the fear of failing at something brand new."

Cami looked over at Shelby. She always seemed so composed, so sure of herself. It was hard to imagine her ever feeling the same doubt Cami felt right now.

"So, how did you deal with it? The fear?"

Shelby smiled softly. "Honestly, I just woke up every day and took it one day at a time. I just took the next right step. That was something my grandmother used to say. When I would get scared at school because I was worried about a test or something along those lines, she would tell me to do the next right thing. Not to think ten steps ahead. Just think about the next right thing. And I also had to remind myself that I was allowed to make mistakes.

That I didn't need to be right all the time. And once I started working at the bookstore and began the book club, I realized how much happier I was. The fear doesn't go away completely, but you don't have to let it control you."

Cami nodded. "I guess that's where I am now. It's that leap part that's scary. You know, jumping off the cliff without a parachute."

Shelby walked over and placed a comforting hand on her shoulder. "You're already in the air, Cami. You took the leap when you signed the lease on this studio. You're leaping every time you roll paint across these walls. You're doing it. You already jumped."

"I guess you're right. I have already jumped."

"Exactly. And trust me, you're going to land just fine."

They continued painting in silence for a few moments. The only sound was the swish of the paint rolling against the wall.

"I've been thinking," Cami said, "maybe I should host an open house once the studio is set up. You know, something small just to invite the neighborhood, show them the space, let them know I'm here. Maybe show some simple yoga poses."

"That's a great idea," Shelby said. "It would be the

perfect way to introduce yourself and the studio. And I'm sure Lacy would help."

"I like that idea. I can make it a little event like with tea and snacks, maybe some raffle prizes for free classes," Cami said.

"Exactly. It'll get people excited, and word of mouth will spread. People love new places like this. They want to support small businesses."

Cami felt the tension in her shoulders ease. "You always know how to make things sound so simple, Shelby."

Shelby laughed. "I guess I'm pretty simple-minded."

"You know that's not what I meant," Cami said, rolling her eyes. "Thanks for coming today. I really needed this."

Shelby nodded. "Anytime. We're all rooting for you."

And Cami knew they were. She had a village around her, a strong support group of women who all had their own problems but who were all there for each other. And there was no better kind of family than that.

CHAPTER 4

SHELBY PULLED into the parking lot of the big box store and turned off the engine. She glanced over at Willadeene, who was sitting beside her in the passenger seat with her arms crossed and her lips pursed in what could only be described as her permanent scowl. Shelby was trying to keep a positive attitude. It was the Christmas holiday season, after all, and she knew this would be an interesting day of shopping with Willadeene.

"Okay, here we are," Shelby said, unbuckling her seat belt and trying to sound excited. "Are you ready to shop for some foster kids?"

Willadeene grunted. "I guess, but don't expect me to be hauling around any of those big plastic toys I know you'll buy. I'm too old for that."

Shelby bit her lip, trying not to laugh. Willadeene wasn't exactly a poster child for holiday cheer, and if it wasn't for the fact that she had nothing else going on today, Shelby doubted she would have even invited her to come along. But she felt sorry for her. It was the second holiday season that she knew her, and Willadeene had no family to spend the holidays with. Her husband had died over fifteen years ago, and they never had any kids. Willadeene never mentioned any other family members either, and since she was part of their neighborhood group, they had to consider her their black sheep of the family. Shelby figured maybe one day she could turn her around and make her a more positive person.

"Don't worry," Shelby said as she climbed out of the car. "You can just supervise from the cart. I'll do the heavy lifting."

Willadeene grunted again as she got out of the car and shuffled towards the store entrance. Shelby followed, grabbing a cart on the way inside. The store was already in full holiday mode. Christmas music played from the overhead sound system, and the aisles were lined with all kinds of festive decorations, gift wraps, and the types of toys that caused chaos on Christmas morning with their beeping and loud sounds.

She pulled out a list of the foster children's wishes, thinking about the joy these gifts would bring on Christmas morning. One of her favorite holiday traditions was shopping for the kids who might not get much otherwise. She had done this even before moving to Charleston. She looked forward to it every year.

"Okay, first on the list," Shelby said, pushing the cart toward the toy section. "We need to get a few things for this eight-year-old girl who loves dolls."

Willadeene rolled her eyes. "Dolls, what a waste. Kids today should be learning useful skills, not just playing with silly dolls."

"Dolls are still popular, and this little girl specifically asked for an interactive one. You know, the ones that talk and say things like, 'Change my diaper,' or 'I'm hungry, feed me.'"

Willadeene scrunched up her nose. "Good Lord, help us. Who thought it was a good idea to make a doll that talked? That's just asking for trouble."

Shelby laughed, knowing that reasoning with Willadeene would be pointless. She pushed the cart down the aisle, grabbing one of the dolls off the shelves. "Here we go, perfect for the eight-year-old little girl."

Willadeene peered at the box as if it were filled

with live snakes. "That thing looks like it's going to come to life in the middle of the night and try to take over the world."

Shelby snorted with laughter. "It's just a doll, Willadeene, I promise."

"Well, you know there's all kinds of haunted things here in the Lowcountry," Willadeene said, a warning tone in her voice.

"I don't believe in that sort of stuff," Shelby replied.

"The ghosts count on that."

They continued down the aisles with Shelby grabbing various items from the list—action figures, stuffed animals, art supplies. Willadeene had a relentless running commentary, but Shelby laughed more than she got frustrated.

"Is this a Nerf gun?" Willadeene said, picking up a brightly colored toy gun. "You're buying this? Do you want these kids running around, shooting each other in the face?"

"It's on the list," Shelby said. "Apparently, Nerf battles are all the rage these days."

Willadeene muttered something under her breath but dropped the item into the cart. "Well, back in my day, we made our own fun. We didn't need fancy gadgets. We played outside with sticks and stones. That's what made us strong."

"Right," Shelby said, grabbing a set of Legos off the shelf. "And that's why you turned out to be so tough, Willadeene."

"You bet your bottom dollar," she replied, lifting her chin slightly as she looked at the rows of toys with disapproval.

They continued moving through the store, filling the cart with gifts. Shelby couldn't help but feel accomplished. Despite Willadeene's grumbling, they were making good progress, and the kids would have a wonderful Christmas. When they reached the clothing section, Shelby paused to check the list again.

"All right, we need some winter jackets for a couple of the older kids."

Willadeene grunted again. "Winter jackets in Charleston? All they need is a good windbreaker and a scarf. That would work just fine."

"Well, I guess they want to be prepared," Shelby said, picking up two puffy jackets and tossing them into the cart. "Besides, you never know when we might get a cold snap."

Willadeene shook her head but didn't say anything else.

As they finished the shopping, the cart was full, and now it was time for lunch. "I don't know about you, but I'm starving," Shelby said, looking at her watch. "How about we go grab something to eat before we head home?"

"Where?" Willadeene asked, raising an eyebrow.

"Well, there's a cute little café down the way, local spot. They've got great sandwiches and coffee."

Willadeene gave her a reluctant nod. "Fine, but don't expect me to eat one of those fancy sandwiches that has goat cheese or sprouts on it. And remember, I hate seafood."

Shelby laughed. "Yes, I remember you hate seafood. You live by the ocean, but you hate seafood."

They checked out, loaded the car, and headed to the café. By the time they walked in, the place was buzzing with the lunch crowd. Shelby looked across the room, trying to find a table, when she saw Reed sitting by the window.

"Hey, there's Reed," she said. "Let's grab a seat with him."

Willadeene grumbled something about third-wheeling but followed Shelby over to the table.

Reed looked up from his menu and smiled, standing to greet them. "Hey, ladies," he said, giving

Shelby a kiss on the cheek. "Fancy meeting you here. How's the shopping going?"

"Exhausting," Shelby said, sliding into the seat across from him. She pasted on a fake smile.

Willadeene sat down with a loud sigh. "That place was a madhouse. You should never go out this time of year."

Reed chuckled and then raised an eyebrow at Shelby. "You holding up okay?"

She gave him a tired smile. "I'm fine, but I need food. My blood sugar is low. Willadeene sure has been keeping me on my toes."

Willadeene was clearly uninterested in this part of the conversation. "I'm going to the bathroom. Don't order for me."

As soon as Willadeene disappeared, Shelby slumped forward, dropping her head into her hands. "Oh my gosh, Reed, she's impossible. I don't know how her husband did it. Every time I picked something up, she would have something to say. Nothing was good enough. She hates all toys, thinks clothing is ridiculous apparently, and don't even get me started about the Nerf gun."

Reed leaned back, laughing. "You signed up for this. She didn't exactly promise that she'd be easygoing."

"I know," Shelby groaned. "I just thought it would be nice for her to get out of the house. Give her something to do, you know. It's the Christmas holidays. I thought she would enjoy it, but she makes everything so hard."

He reached across the table and squeezed her hand. "And you're a saint for putting up with her. Literally, I think God is writing something down in your permanent record right now. She doesn't have anyone else, and you know how much she likes to complain. This gives her something to talk about."

"I just wish she'd be a little more festive."

Reed smiled. "She's not built for festive, honey, but you are, and you're making Christmas better for a lot of kids. You have to focus on that."

"Thanks. You're right, as usual."

At that moment, Willadeene returned, her face twisted in annoyance. "This place needs some serious work. No paper towels in the bathroom, and the door sticks."

Shelby raised an eyebrow at Reed, stifling a laugh. "We'll be sure to file a complaint," she said lightly.

Willadeene sat down with a huff, adjusting her coat. "Anyway, let's order. I'm starving."

Shelby smiled at Reed, shaking her head. Just another day with Willadeene.

"The service in this place is slower than molasses," she said, reaching for her water. "I swear, I could have gone somewhere else today and gotten better service."

Shelby looked over at Reed, biting back a smile. Willadeene had always had something to complain about, but she seemed more irritable today than usual. Still, they hadn't been waiting all that long.

"We haven't even ordered yet," Shelby said. "I'm sure it'll pick up once we do."

"Uh-huh," Willadeene said, taking a sip of her water. She stared at the menu with visible displeasure. "I've been to better places."

Shelby raised an eyebrow, sensing something else going on behind Willadeene's grumbling today. "You know, you've been a little bit off today," she said, trying to keep a light tone. "Is everything okay?"

Willadeene sniffed, her expression hardening. "I'm fine. I'm just not in the mood to deal with slow waitresses and noisy children running around toy store aisles."

"You don't seem like yourself, Willadeene. Are you sure nothing's bothering you?" Reed asked.

Her lips pressed into a tight line. Shelby thought

she saw some kind of flicker in her eyes, an unease that hadn't been there before. Then, just as quickly, her defensive walls went up again.

"I said I'm fine," she snapped, folding her arms. "It's nothing you two need to worry about."

Shelby frowned. Willadeene was always grumpy, but this felt different. She seemed concerned about something. "If something's going on, you know you can talk to us. We are your friends, Willadeene."

For a brief second, Willadeene's expression wavered a bit. Her eyes darted down to the table. Shelby saw a hesitation, but then she shook her head and muttered, "It's nothing."

Shelby exchanged a quick glance with Reed. He noticed it, too. Willadeene wasn't just irritated today; she was distracted by something.

"Come on, Willadeene," Shelby coaxed, leaning in. "It's not like you to keep things bottled up. You say whatever you're thinking. What's going on?"

Willadeene stared at her water glass for a long moment and then finally sighed, her shoulders slumping forward a little. "If you must know, I got a letter." Her voice was barely audible.

Shelby blinked. "A letter? From who?"

Willadeene's jaw clenched tightly. "It was from my sister."

Shelby's eyes widened. Willadeene had never talked about any extended family. Shelby had always assumed she had no living relatives. "Your sister? I didn't even know you had a sister."

"Well, there's a good reason for that," Willadeene said in a sharp tone. "We haven't spoken in over thirty years, and I plan on keeping it that way."

Shelby's heart broke. Thirty years? That was a long time to hold a grudge, even for somebody like Willadeene. "What happened?"

For a moment, it looked like Willadeene might shut down the conversation entirely. She let out a frustrated sigh, looking over at Shelby with a mixture of irritation and something that bordered on vulnerability.

"It's none of your business," she snapped, but her words lacked their usual force. "But if you must know, she wrote to me. That's all. Wants to make amends or some such nonsense. I crumpled it up and threw it in the drawer. When I get home, it's going in the trash can where it belongs."

Shelby's heart twisted in a knot. She had never seen Willadeene so rattled. Her tough exterior, the constant complaining—it was all still there, but there was something fragile underneath all of that today. She needed to tread carefully.

"Maybe she really does want to make things right. Maybe it's worth hearing her out," Shelby said gently.

Willadeene scoffed, her face hardening into stone again. "After what she did? No, thank you. Some things can't be fixed, and I don't need you trying to help me figure it out."

Shelby opened her mouth to ask exactly what happened, but Willadeene's sharp look silenced her in her tracks. She knew pushing too hard right now was not a good idea.

"Okay, I'm not going to continue prying, but if you want to talk about it, I'm here for you, and I'm sure Joan, Cami, and Lacy would be too."

Willadeene stared out the window. Shelby knew she had struck a nerve. Whether she liked it or not, that letter bothered her more than she wanted to admit out loud.

Finally, the waitress appeared to take their orders, and the tension at the table broke just enough. Willadeene ordered a sandwich and then complained about it being too dry, but Shelby didn't mind. She just wanted to keep the conversation light. She shifted the focus back to Christmas shopping and wedding planning, but Willadeene was quiet for the rest of the time they were together.

She had a sister. It must have been a very deep wound to be apart when that was her only living relative.

"You know, it's never too late to make things right," Shelby said when they pulled into the driveway back home.

Willadeene didn't say anything, but Shelby hoped that maybe Christmas would bring more than just gifts for the foster children. Maybe it would bring Willadeene and her family back, too.

Joan sat cross-legged on her living room floor, a half-filled box of keepsakes sitting in front of her. She reached for a framed photo of her and Andrew from their early days as a couple, their faces full of love and life. Her fingers traced across the edge of the wooden frame as she let out a soft sigh. This house had been *their* house. It had been home for so long. She knew every inch of it, like the back of her hand, and now, as she was preparing to say goodbye, it seemed impossible.

The real estate agent was coming soon to look at the house before listing it. They wanted to give her an idea of the price she could expect to get and what she needed to do to get it ready for sale after the first of the year. It made her stomach twist into a knot to think about walking out of there one day and never going back. She wasn't just selling her house; she was closing a chapter of her life that had been full of every emotion, from love to grief to growth.

Her eyes wandered to the backyard through the living room window. There was the old wooden swing Andrew had built that still hung from a large oak tree. She could hear his voice calling her outside that weekend afternoon, proudly announcing, "Look what I've made for us, Joanie." They'd spent hours together on that swing, laughing and talking under the shade of the live oak tree. It was one of those simple things that had made this house a home. The memories tugged at her heart, bringing a bittersweet smile to her face.

She looked at the bookshelf on the opposite wall. That was another of Andrew's projects. It was sturdy, made with his own two hands. Every screw had been driven in with care. She laughed softly, remembering how he had insisted on building it himself despite not having much experience with carpentry. The shelves were still slightly crooked, but she loved it that way. It was perfectly imperfect, just like Andrew had been.

She turned her head and saw the bathroom in her line of sight. She could almost see that gouge in the tile near the sink, a reminder of the time he had dropped his glass of water and cursed under his breath. She had made fun of him, telling him he was clumsy, and they had both laughed as they cleaned up the mess. Of course, there were bad times with his drinking problem, but there were also so many good times that she could remember, that she *preferred* to remember.

She ran her fingers through her hair as she sighed. This house had witnessed many moments like that—moments of joy, love, and loss. He'd been gone for years now, but his presence still lingered in every corner of this home they had shared. It was hard to believe that she was going to leave it all behind and that somebody else was going to live here and make their own memories. The memories she had would be hers alone, unknown to the people who lived here next.

She returned the photo to the box and reached for the next item. As much as she was looking forward to being near her son and grandchild, the thought of leaving Waverly Lane gave her a quiet ache in her stomach. The friendships she had formed here in the last year had become like a second family to her, a sanctuary, and now all of that would change.

A knock at the door broke her out of her daydream. She blinked, glancing at the clock. It wasn't time for the real estate agent yet. She got up and wiped her hands on her jeans before walking to the door.

When she opened it, Randy stood on the other side with a small bouquet of flowers. His smile was warm.

"Hey there," he said, stepping inside. "I thought you might need a little pick-me-up."

She smiled, feeling her heart lighten at the sight of him. She had never thought she would have a second chance at love. Her love with Randy was strong and true, but it was different than what she had with Andrew. She had learned that it was okay to have two different types of love. They were equally as real and as strong.

"You always know how to make me feel better," she said, taking the flowers and kissing him on the cheek. She walked to the kitchen and grabbed a vase to put them in. As she arranged them, Randy leaned against the counter, watching her.

"How's the packing going?"

She shrugged, putting the vase in the middle of

the kitchen table. "It's going. I've been getting senti-
mental about just about everything in this house.
Every corner has a memory of Andrew. That swing
in the backyard, that bookshelf over there."

He nodded, stepping closer, wrapping an arm
around her shoulders, pulling her gently to his side.
"I get it. You've been here a long time. Starting over
doesn't mean forgetting. Andrew will always be a
part of you, no matter where you go. You're not
leaving the memories behind. You're taking those
with you, too."

She leaned into him, thankful for his steady presence. "I know," she said. "It's just hard. This place has
been my home for so long. It's where we built our
life together, where I grieved when he was gone, and
where I started over again. I'm excited to be near my
son and to watch my grandson grow up, but I sure
wish I didn't have to leave Waverly Lane to do it."

His hand rubbed small circles on her back. "I
know it's hard. This isn't the end of something. It's
the beginning. You've got so much life ahead of you,
Joan. Being near your son and being part of Andy's
life, that's going to be a blessing. We'll figure all of
this out together. You're not doing this alone."

Randy had been her rock this past year,
supporting her through everything.

"I know you're right," she said. "It's just... I guess I didn't expect to feel this sad about it. This house is so full of memories, but maybe it's time to make new ones."

"That's right, and those new memories are going to be just as special as the old ones."

The two of them stood there for a moment, wrapped in each other's warmth, before Joan gently pulled away and looked at the boxes stacked around the room.

"I should probably finish packing these before the agent gets here. Want to help?"

He nodded. "Of course, anything you need."

CHAPTER 5

SHELBY SAT on the floor in front of her giant Christmas tree, adjusting one of the ornaments. The multicolored lights twinkled gently. She listened as Nat King Cole's voice crooned softly in the background, singing her favorite tune during the holidays called "The Christmas Song." It blended seamlessly with the crackling of the fire. It was late November, and despite the storm gathering strength outside, the inside of her home felt like a cozy holiday haven from a movie.

She heard the sound of Reed's car pulling into the driveway and stood up, smoothing her red sweater down as she made her way to the front door. When she opened it, a gust of wind nearly knocked her off her feet, bringing with it a chilly rush of air that was uncommon during this time of the year in Charleston.

Reed stood there with a large takeout bag in one hand and a bouquet in the other.

"Well, don't you look festive," he said, stepping inside as quickly as possible before the wind blew the Christmas tree across the house. "Is that Nat King Cole I hear?"

She laughed, helping him off with his coat and kissing his cheek. "It's my favorite Christmas song. I wanted everything to feel special tonight, make a real event of it."

Reed handed her the bouquet. "I brought you your favorite straight from the restaurant."

Shelby's eyes lit up as she took the flowers and peeked into the takeout bag. The scent of country-fried steak, mashed potatoes, and fresh bread wafted out, making her mouth water instantly.

"Reed, this is perfect. You didn't have to go all out like this."

He shrugged, walking into the living room and admiring the Christmas decorations on the mantle she had so carefully decorated. "Of course I did. It's not every night we get to enjoy dinner by the tree, with the wind howling like we're at the North Pole."

She followed him, putting the flowers in a vase

and placing them on the dining table, which had already been laid out with plates and candles. Her eyes flicked toward the window, and she noticed the wind had picked up even more. The branches of the old oak tree in the backyard swayed ominously.

"I guess it's good we're staying in tonight," she said. "Though I do feel like we're in one of those Hallmark movies where the storm keeps the couple stranded inside together."

He laughed as he unpacked the bag of takeout from his restaurant. "If we're in a Hallmark movie, we need more snow and less wind."

"Well, we'll give it an hour. With this weather, we might get both."

They sat down at the table with the glow of the Christmas tree illuminating the room. The music from the old holiday station added a little nostalgia to the moment.

Shelby found herself staring over at Reed when he wasn't looking. It was hard to believe that in a few weeks, they would be standing at the altar and saying their vows. He reached across the table, taking her hand in his.

"You did an amazing job with these decorations. This place feels like Christmas exploded but in the best possible way."

She laughed. "Well, I love going all out for the holidays. And it's our first Christmas together as a married couple, at least for Christmas Day. I wanted everything to feel extra special."

They had decided they would move into Shelby's house after the wedding because she was so attached to her Waverly Lane friends and her book club. Reed didn't have any special attachment to his very large apartment.

"Everything does feel extra special," he said. "I love this. I love that we get to build these traditions together."

Her heart swelled at his words. Her ex-husband had never said things like that. Before she could respond, the wind outside picked up again. It howled loudly, rattling the windows. She hadn't realized how fierce this storm was going to become.

"It's getting worse out there," she said. "Do you think it'll knock out the power?"

He shrugged, taking a bite of mashed potatoes. "Maybe. But even if it does, we'll be okay. We've got candles, a nice fire, and each other. What more do we need?"

As if on cue, the house suddenly plunged into darkness. The hum of the refrigerator stopped, the music cut out mid-song, and the only thing left was the flickering of the fire and the soft glow that it sent across the room.

"Well," she said, giggling, "I guess that answers that."

Reed reached for a lighter on the table and quickly lit the candles she'd placed. The soft flames danced in the darkness. Shelby couldn't help but feel the magic of the moment.

"There we go," he said, settling back into his chair. "Dinner by candlelight? That stepped things up a notch, I would say."

She took a sip of her wine. "You know, I kind of like this. It's like the universe is telling us to slow down and enjoy this moment."

He raised his glass in agreement. "To unexpected moments and slowing down."

They clinked glasses and continued eating, chatting about this and that—everything from Christmas plans to wedding details to Willadeene. The storm continued raging outside, but inside, time had slowed down, and the rest of the world didn't matter.

"You don't think this storm's going to cause any damage to the house, do you?"

He looked out the window. "I doubt it. This

house is solid. It's been here forever. These aren't hurricane-force winds or anything."

She nodded, focusing back on her meal. "I guess we'll just have to trust that everything's going to be fine, no matter what. We have bigger things to focus on, like getting married in a few weeks."

"That's right, and no matter what happens, as long as we're together, everything's going to work out," Reed said.

They finished the rest of their meal by candle-light as the storm swirled outside. After dinner, they cleared the table together, washed the dishes, and then stood in front of the fire. He pulled her into his arms.

"You know," he said, brushing a strand of stray hair behind her ear, "I wouldn't mind more nights like this."

She smiled, resting her head against his chest. "Me neither, but without the storm next time. That part can be eliminated."

"That part can be eliminated," he chuckled. "Deal. Storm or no storm, I wouldn't trade this moment with you for anything."

Shelby stood behind the counter at the bookstore, stacking a fresh pile of new books and humming softly to the Christmas music playing over the speakers. The afternoon had been quiet, with only a handful of loyal customers coming in to browse. The storm had been so bad last night that many people were dealing with fallen trees at their own houses.

She didn't mind quiet days at the bookstore. It gave her more time to read and be with her thoughts. It also gave her time to organize the shelves and plan the rest of the day. She looked up at the clock—just a couple more hours of work before she was going to head home and curl up with a book of her own.

The bell above the door jingled, signaling that somebody had arrived. She looked up, expecting to see one of her regulars, but saw Reed walking in instead. At first, she smiled, but then she saw that his face didn't look quite right, that he was wringing his hands a bit, something he only did when he was nervous.

"Reed?" she asked, her voice laced with concern as she stepped out from behind the counter. "What's wrong?"

He looked around the shop like he was trying to find the right words. His expression gave him away.

Something was very, very wrong. Her stomach dropped as she walked over to him quickly, touching his arm.

"Reed, talk to me. What happened?"

He swallowed hard, his jaw clenched when he finally met her eyes. "Shelby," he said, his voice a bit unsteady. "I just drove by the church."

She blinked, her heart racing. "The church? What about it?"

He hesitated, looking like he was trying to find any way to soften the blow. "It's just, there's been damage, a lot of damage."

Shelby's breath felt like it was caught in her throat. "What kind of damage?"

He sighed, running his hand through his hair. "That storm last night knocked down a huge tree. It fell right on the roof of the church. It collapsed a huge part of the roof, Shelby."

Her eyes widened, her hand instinctively going over her mouth. "Oh no, is everyone okay?"

"Yeah, nobody was there when it happened, thankfully," he said, his face still tight with worry. "But again, the damage is bad. I got out of my car and spoke to the pastor. He said it's going to take a few months to repair. The church won't be able to host our wedding."

She stared at him like the weight of the words had to sink into her chest. "What do you mean? We can't get married there?"

His eyes softened as he stepped closer, taking her hands in his. "I'm so sorry. I know how much you loved that place. But the pastor said there's no way they'll get it fixed in time. We have to find another venue."

She felt a wave of nausea wash over her. The church, that beautiful historic church where she had imagined walking down the aisle and dreamed of since she got engaged, wasn't going to be her wedding venue anymore. Just like that, the wedding was weeks away, and now they didn't even have a place to get married.

"I don't understand," she said, her mind racing. "How could this happen? I thought we had everything under control."

He squeezed her hands, speaking softly and steadily. "I know, but we don't control Mother Nature. This is a shock, but we're going to figure it out. We still have time. There are other places we can look at—"

"But not like the church," she said, interrupting him. "It was perfect, Reed. It was everything I wanted."

Tears threatened to spill out the corners of her eyes. He pulled her into his arms, holding her tightly, allowing the reality of the situation to sink in. She stood there with her head resting against his chest, feeling the warmth, but her heart ached.

"I'm so sorry, honey," he said, stroking her hair. "I wish I could fix this. I wish I could make it all go away."

She took a deep breath to steady herself. "I just... I don't know what we're going to do now. There's no time to find another place, and I don't want just some generic venue."

He looked down at her. "Listen to me. We're getting married no matter what happens. That's what's important. We'll figure out the details. I promise it'll be just as beautiful, even if it's not at the church."

"I know, I just... I don't want to settle for something that doesn't feel special. This was supposed to be perfect."

"And it will be," he said firmly. "We're in this together. We're going to make it work."

She took in another breath and breathed it out slowly. "Okay. We'll figure it out. But we need to come up with a plan—very quickly."

He smiled, brushing a tear from her cheek.

"There's my lady. We'll make some calls and check out a few places. I even called a couple of venues on the way over here to see if anything was available."

She raised an eyebrow. "You did?"

He nodded. "Yeah, I didn't want to worry you until I knew what was happening. I'm just waiting for callbacks."

"You really are the best, you know that?" she said, touching his cheek.

He leaned down and pressed a soft kiss to her forehead. "Just trying to keep my bride happy."

Shelby sat at Lacy's kitchen table, feeling an anxiety she couldn't remember ever feeling in her life. They had lost their venue. She didn't know what she was going to do. The sound of Lacy's laptop keys clicking away was the only thing breaking the silence as they scrolled through endless websites, desperately searching for a new place to hold the wedding. Everything seemed hopeless.

Reed sat beside Shelby, his hand resting gently on her knee. The weight of the situation hung over them like a dark cloud. The Christmas tree twinkled with beautiful white lights in the corner of Lacy's living room. It was perfect, like something out of a magazine—so different from how Shelby's tree looked, covered in mismatched family heirloom ornaments. The trees were a reminder that the holiday season was fast approaching and, with it, their wedding date. Yet now everything seemed so uncertain.

"Nope," Lacy said, letting out a frustrated sigh. She leaned back in her chair and ran a hand through her hair. "That one's booked too. I called them this morning. They don't have anything until the end of January, at the earliest."

Shelby groaned and buried her face in her hands. "Of course they don't. Why would any decent venue be available this close to Christmas?"

Lacy glanced at Reed, her expression sympathetic. She didn't have an answer. Nobody did. The storm that had knocked a tree onto the roof of the historic church had ruined all their plans. Now, they were scrambling to find an alternative with just a little less than three weeks until the wedding. Every phone call and every search had turned up nothing. No venue was available on such short notice during the holiday season, and if it was, it probably wasn't a place Shelby wanted for her wedding.

"We'll find something," Reed said, gently

squeezing Shelby's knee. "We just have to keep look-ing. We could always use the restaurant."

Shelby looked at him, confused. "The restaurant? It's not nearly big enough for something like this. Plus, you'd have to close down to have our wedding, and Christmas Eve is one of your busiest days of the year."

"But if I need to close it, I will—"

"No, Reed," she interrupted, shaking her head. "We're not doing that. Some families depend on having their Christmas Eve dinner there."

Shelby lifted her head, her eyes filled with frus-tration. "We've been looking and nothing. Every place we've called is either booked, too small, or just... not right. Maybe we should go to the justice of the peace and get it over with."

Reed squeezed her hand. "I know that's just your frustration talking."

Shelby pushed back from the table and stood up, pacing across Lacy's kitchen. "You know, maybe this is a sign. Maybe we just need to postpone the wedding. It's too much—trying to find a new venue this close to the date. I'd rather wait than settle for something that doesn't feel right."

Reed's face tightened. He stood and walked toward her, his voice firm but gentle. "Shelby, no.

We're not postponing the wedding. We've been planning this for months. We can't let a tree falling on the church stop us from getting married."

Shelby crossed her arms, her eyes brimming with tears. "But what if we can't find a place? What if we're forced to settle for some venue that doesn't feel like us? I don't want a random, quick wedding. I want it to be special."

"It will be special," Reed said, stepping closer, his voice soft. "Because we'll be together, and that's the most important thing."

She blew out a slow breath, but the tension in her shoulders refused to ease. She looked across the room at the Christmas lights, trying to focus on their glow, wishing things could go back to how they were before the storm. She had imagined her wedding day so many times, walking down the aisle of that beautiful old church. It was the one place she and Reed had immediately fallen in love with. And now, that whole plan was gone.

Lacy, who had been sitting quietly, allowing them to talk, cleared her throat. "You know," she said slowly, "there is another option."

Shelby and Reed turned to look at her. "What option?" Shelby asked, her tone skeptical.

"Your backyard."

Shelby blinked. "My backyard?"

Lacy nodded. "Yeah, it's big enough. You've got that beautiful garden space, and we could rent a huge tent. That way, rain or shine, the wedding will go off without a hitch."

Shelby shook her head, the idea instantly making her heart sink. "No, Lacy, I don't want an outdoor wedding. That's not what we planned."

"I know it's not what you planned," Lacy said, leaning forward in her chair, "but it's an option, and honestly, it could be beautiful. We can decorate the tent with twinkle lights, make it feel cozy and elegant. You wouldn't have to worry about finding a last-minute venue. It's going to save you a ton of money. Your house is right there, and it's convenient. We can make it special. Every time you look out into your backyard, you'll remember your wedding day."

Reed's hand tightened around Shelby's. "Lacy's right. We can make the backyard work. We'll rent a tent and hire someone to decorate it however you want. It may not be perfect or what you originally thought, but it'll be ours."

Shelby's heart twisted in her chest. She still had that perfect wedding day vision running through her mind. But now, she was running out of time and options. She wanted to marry Reed more than anything, but giving up her dream wedding felt like defeat.

"I don't know," she said softly, shaking her head. "It just doesn't feel right. I never imagined an outdoor wedding."

Lacy stood up and walked over, putting a hand on Shelby's shoulder. "I get it. I do. Sometimes, things don't go as planned, and you just have to roll with it. What matters most is that you and Reed are getting married on Christmas Eve. Everything else? It's just details. I promise we'll make your backyard beautiful. You won't even recognize it. When you walk down that aisle, it'll feel special. I'll make sure of it."

Shelby looked at her friend, letting Lacy's words sink in. This might not be the dream wedding she had envisioned, but she needed to focus more on the dream marriage she would have with Reed.

"Okay," she said quietly. "Let's do it. Let's use the backyard."

Reed's face broke into a relieved smile, and he hugged her tightly. "Are you sure?"

Shelby nodded against his chest. "Yeah, I just want to get married. I don't care if it's in the backyard or at some fancy venue. I want to marry you, Reed, and that's all that matters."

Lacy grinned, her excitement bubbling up. "You won't regret this, Shelby. We're going to make it amazing, I promise."

Shelby wiped away the few lingering tears and smiled at both of them. "Okay. Let's get started then. We have a lot of work to do."

CHAPTER 6

WILLADEENE SAT in her worn armchair, watching as her favorite soap opera, Everlasting Hearts, played in the background. The characters she had followed for years were on the screen, with their dramatic declarations of love and betrayal. However, her focus was elsewhere. She had a half-finished crossword puzzle sitting in her lap and was tapping her pencil against the edge of the page as she stared at it.

"Four-letter word for betrayal," she muttered to herself, chewing on the end of her pencil. "Lies? No, that doesn't work. Maybe..."

The sudden ring of her phone cut through her concentration, causing her to jump. Willadeene frowned, looking at the phone on the small table beside her. Nobody ever called her at this time of day. She usually didn't get phone calls unless they were from scammers or the wrong number. She hesitated a moment before reluctantly picking up the receiver.

"Hello?" she said, her tone sharp.

At first, there was nothing but silence. Her frown deepened as she waited, gripping the phone tighter. "I don't have time for prank calls," she snapped. "Who is this?"

Just as she was about to hang up, she heard someone speaking softly.

"Willadeene?"

Her breath caught in her throat. She had not heard that voice in years but would recognize it anywhere. It was a voice she thought she'd never hear again.

"Willadeene, are you there?"

She gripped the phone so tightly that her fingers were turning white, her heart pounding in her chest, which was hard to do given that she was on beta blockers that kept her heart rate down.

"Gertie." It was a statement, not a question.

There was a pause on the other end as if Gertie was unsure what to say next. Willadeene's stomach twisted in a knot. She felt bitterness and anger rising inside of her. She'd held on to it for so long that it was always bubbling right there at the top.

"I didn't think you'd pick up," Gertie finally said.

Willadeene's jaw clenched so hard that she was afraid she might break her dentures. "What do you want?"

"I've been trying to reach you. I sent a letter, actually a couple of letters. Did you get them?"

"I got them," Willadeene said coolly. Her voice was as cold as the ice packs in her freezer, "and I threw them away, just like I'm about to hang up this phone."

"Willadeene, please—"

"Why are you calling me now, after all this time?" Willadeene said, cutting her off. "What in the world could you possibly have to say after thirty years of not speaking?"

There was a long pause. Willadeene even thought Gertie might have hung up, but then her voice came through again, quieter.

"I just... I wanted to talk. I've been thinking about you and about us. It's been too long."

Willadeene's chest tightened, and she worried that she might need to call the ambulance. She wasn't about to let Gertie's words get to her and cause a heart attack, not after the hurt and the betrayal.

"It's been too long because *you* made it that way," Willadeene said. "You chose to walk away, and you know what you did. Don't you act like you're the victim here."

"I'm not trying to—"

"Then what are you trying to do?" Willadeene said, interrupting. "Because I moved on, Gertie. I don't need you calling me up out of the blue pretending like we're sisters, like we can just fix things."

"I'm not pretending," Gertie said. "I know things went wrong between us, but—"

"Went wrong?" Willadeene said, interrupting her again. "I guess that's one way to put it. I don't have time for these shenanigans. Whatever it is that you're after this time, I'm not interested."

Gertie sat there silently. Willadeene could hear the faint sound of her shaky, uneven breathing.

"I just want to see you," Gertie finally said. "I thought maybe we could meet, just once, to talk. I've missed you, Willadeene. We were very close at one time."

Willadeene felt a pang deep in her chest that she tried to ignore. She wasn't going to fall for this. She had been through too much and carried the weight of their history for far too long.

"I don't think so," Willadeene said firmly. "There is nothing left to talk about. I made peace with this a long time ago."

That wasn't really true.

"Please," Gertie said again, "just one time. We could have coffee. It doesn't have to be—"

"I said no," Willadeene snapped, her voice shaking now. She hated it when emotions came up. She kept them pushed down as tight as she could. She squeezed her eyes shut, trying to force the feelings back deep inside her. "I don't want to see you, Gertie. I'm fine without you. I always have been."

There was another long, heavy silence on the other end. Willadeene didn't know why she didn't just hang up the phone. She had the power to do that. Maybe it was her curiosity.

"I'm sorry," Gertie said, just above a whisper, "for everything."

Willadeene's throat tightened. She wasn't going to let herself give in. She couldn't, not after all those years and not after what happened. Without saying another word, she hung up the phone. She sat there for a minute with her hands still on it, half believing that Gertie would call right back, but she didn't.

The TV droned on, and Willadeene had no idea what was happening with her soap opera. Her eyes drifted to another unopened letter from Gertie sitting on the table. She reached for it, crumpled it, and threw it in the trash can beside her recliner. She had spent three decades building walls around herself, and now, with just one phone call, Gertie was trying to tear it all down.

She swallowed hard and told herself that she didn't need her sister. She'd gotten along just fine without her for all these years. She looked back down at her crossword puzzle, but it was useless. Her mind was a swirl of questions, and she just couldn't concentrate on it.

Shelby stood in her kitchen with a pile of freshly baked sugar cookies cooling on the counter. The scent of cinnamon and vanilla permeated the air. Christmas music played softly in the background, a mix of classics and contemporary, and her tree twinkled from the foyer, its twelve-foot height creating a colorful glow throughout the house. She looked over her shoulder to make sure everything was set up for the evening, wiping her hands on her vintage

Christmas-themed apron. The kitchen was covered in bowls of icing, sprinkles, and an array of cookie cutters in every shape imaginable. She had spent the day baking the cookies, and they would probably end up baking more before the evening was over.

The doorbell rang, and Shelby hurried to open it for her friends. "Come on in!" she called out, wiping her hands again. "I've got the cookies all ready to decorate. Well, at least the first batch."

As usual, Lacy was the first of her friends through the door, carrying a tin of peppermint bark she'd made earlier. "I come bearing gifts," she said, handing the tin to Shelby. "I figured we'd need something to snack on so we don't eat the cookies instead of decorating them."

Shelby laughed, putting the tin on the kitchen counter. "The cookies are cooling, we've got all the icing and sprinkles ready, so come on in and grab an apron."

Shelby had bought several aprons at a local shop. She wanted to make this a really fun annual event.

"Tell me how you came up with this idea again?" Cami asked.

"Well, we lived near the local fire station when I was a kid. My mom would always have me invite some friends over for a Christmas cookie decorating party a couple of weeks before Christmas. We would decorate what seemed like hundreds of cookies and deliver them to the fire station. Those guys were always so appreciative. Plus, they always gave us a tour of the fire station and let us ride up high in the ladder truck bucket."

"That's really cool. If I ever have any kids, I'm definitely going to do this with them," Cami said.

"Hey, this is my new annual event. You can bring your kids here," Shelby said, laughing.

"I also brought some holiday trail mix. It's gluten-free and has no added sugar," Cami said, handing her the bowl.

Shelby raised an eyebrow. "No offense, Cami, but we're decorating sugar cookies tonight. I think we've all moved past the healthy snack stage."

"Fair point, but it's here if anyone feels guilty later."

Joan arrived next, with Willadeene following behind her.

"I thought you might want to add these to your tree," Joan said, handing Shelby a festive box of ornaments. "I found them while I was packing, and I don't need them anymore."

Shelby's smile faltered slightly as she took the box. She had been trying not to think about Joan moving away, but she quickly recovered and pulled her in for a hug. "Thank you. I'll find someplace to put them on the tree, and I'll always think of you when I use them every year."

Willadeene arrived bundled in a scarf and sweater, even though Charleston evenings were barely cool enough for a light jacket. She walked inside with a dramatic sigh. "I hope these cookies are worth it. I'm not much of a baker myself."

"You don't have to bake, Willadeene," Shelby said, laughing. "Just slather some icing on them and call it a day."

Once everyone had settled in, the kitchen buzzed with chatter and laughter. The table was spread with bowls of icing in every color—red, white, green, and even blue for the more creative types. Shelby provided sprinkles, tiny candy decorations, and glittery sugar crystals.

"Okay, ladies," Shelby said. "Let's get these cookies looking festive for our local firefighters."

Lacy tied on an apron, eyeing the cookies with a smirk. "Well, don't expect any works of art from me. I'm wonderful with words but not much of an artist."

"That's okay," Cami said, reaching for the piping bag. "I plan to make mine look like they belong in a bakery or maybe even on Pinterest."

Joan laughed as she grabbed one of the star-shaped cookies. "I think you're setting yourself up for disappointment, but I'm here for it."

Willadeene sat on a chair at the table with her arms crossed. "I never understood the fuss over cookies. They all taste the same, no matter what you stick on top of them."

"You just wait, Willadeene," Shelby said. "By the end of the night, you're going to be a cookie-decorating professional."

Each of them grabbed a cookie and started spreading icing, sprinkling sugar, and creating their own designs. Lacy seemed quieter than usual, lost in her thoughts as she focused on her cookies.

"So…" Cami said, looking over at Lacy. "You've been awfully quiet over there. What's going on?"

Lacy looked up. "Oh, nothing," she said. "Just caught up in holiday stress. That's how it is when you have kids."

"Holiday stress? You, Miss Perfect Planner, are stressed?" Shelby said.

"Believe it or not, I get frazzled, especially when I'm buying Christmas presents for my kids and planning somebody's wedding," she said, smirking.

"Well, it's good that you're here. We all need a little distraction from the craziness of the season, and we're doing something good for our local fire-fighters at the same time."

"Come on, Lacy," Cami said, nudging her. "What is going on with you? When are you going to spill it?"

Lacy hesitated, looking around the table at the expectant faces of her friends. She shook her head. "Nothing major. I told you, it's just the usual chaos."

"Well, when you decide you want to vent or share the news with us, we'll all be here," Shelby said.

The conversation shifted to Shelby and Reed getting married in the backyard. Each of the women had their own ideas about what would be good for a wedding in that situation. But then there was Willadeene.

"Well, I think the whole thing sounds like a stupid idea."

"Willadeene, do you have any ability to keep your mouth shut?" Lacy said, wagging her finger.

"Well, I'm just being honest. Getting married in your backyard? Why don't you just get married in your bathroom?"

Shelby couldn't help but laugh at that. "I think I'll stick with the backyard."

As they continued working on their cookies, the women shared stories about different Christmas memories from their childhoods. Shelby talked about how her mother always hosted these cookie parties, but one year, she accidentally put salt out instead of sugar and made the worst-tasting cookies Shelby had ever tried. "The firemen had to get cookies from the grocery store that year."

Cami talked about a holiday yoga retreat she tried to host one year when she first started as a teacher. "Half the class passed out from exhaustion after doing a particularly intense series of poses. Nobody ever wanted to come to one of my holiday retreats again," she laughed.

Joan shared a memory of her late husband, Andrew. "One year, he surprised me by building a wooden sleigh for our front yard. He worked on it every night for a month. I had no idea. It was a wonderful surprise until I sat in it, and the whole seat fell out, hitting the ground." Everybody laughed at the image.

Even Willadeene seemed to soften a bit. "Well, I don't have any heartwarming Christmas stories," she said, returning to her gruff self. "I do remember one year when my sister and I—" She stopped herself. The words hung in the air awkwardly.

Shelby looked up from her cookie. "What about your sister, Willadeene?"

"Nothing," she said quickly. "Never mind."

An awkward silence followed. Shelby knew better than to push Willadeene too hard.

"I was thinking that maybe we could donate a batch of these cookies to the foster care charity we're helping with gifts for," Shelby suggested, breaking the tension.

"That's a great idea, Shelby. The kids will love them," Joan said.

Cami, who had been trying to make a delicate snowflake cookie, looked up in defeat. "Well, they're getting this cookie that looks more like a blob than a snowflake, but it's the thought that counts, right?"

Everybody laughed, and soon, they were all back to decorating their cookies and joking around. Surprisingly, Willadeene had taken to the task, though her cookies didn't look quite so artistic. She accidentally knocked over a bowl of sprinkles, and the colorful bits scattered across the table.

Shelby, Cami, and Lacy all looked at each other, and before they knew it, they were flicking the sprinkles at each other, giggling like children. Even Joan got in on the action, throwing a handful at Cami, who ducked just in time.

Once the cookie decorating was complete and the table was filled with brightly colored treats, they gathered in the living room with cups of hot chocolate. Cookies were piled high on a plate, and they decided to share the extras—the ones that didn't make the cut, the ones too embarrassing to give to anybody.

"You did a good job, Willadeene," Joan said.

Willadeene grunted. "I'm not saying I enjoyed it, but it wasn't the worst thing I've ever done."

"Well, that's high praise," Shelby said with a laugh. "Maybe next year, we'll get you to make some cookies from scratch and bring them over."

"Let's not get ahead of ourselves," Willadeene said, sipping her cocoa.

Shelby was thankful for this group of women. No matter what happened in life or how crazy things got, these women had become her family.

"Okay, ladies, before you all leave, let's take a picture in front of the tree holding up the plates of cookies. This is our first cookie party. This is our first year. It's going to be a tradition."

Joan looked sad. "Well, it'll be a tradition for some of you."

"Maybe you can come visit us when we do it," Shelby said, reaching over and taking her hand.

"That's a nice thought, honey, but Utah is a long way from South Carolina."

They gathered around the tree, holding their cookies. Shelby set up her phone to take a group photo. The Christmas lights twinkled behind them.

"Say Merry Christmas!" Shelby said.

They all chimed in unison, smiling broadly as the camera clicked. This was definitely going to be a Christmas to remember.

Cami stood at the entrance of her new yoga studio, *Twisted*, nervously fiddling with the hem of her green yoga top. The large plate glass windows facing the street were decorated with frosted snowflake decals and snowmen, a nod to the Christmas season despite Charleston's mild winter. The space was lit with soft, warm lighting from hanging lanterns and twinkle lights that she had strung across the walls. The scent of peppermint tea and cinnamon rolls wafted through the air, adding a festive, cozy touch to the atmosphere.

In the corner, she had decorated a small Christmas tree that twinkled with tiny white lights and small ornaments. A table near the entrance held snacks and refreshments: gingerbread cookies, fruit platters, and, of course, hot chocolate with all the fixings. Cami wanted to keep things simple yet inviting for her open house. She hoped the space would give off the welcoming, tranquil vibe she envisioned.

The sign above the door, hand-painted in elegant script, read *Twisted* in a soft green and white hue. The studio felt fresh and modern. This was her big night, the open house to introduce her studio to the community just in time for the holidays. She even had gift certificates ready for those who wanted to give classes to friends or family during the Christmas season.

But now that the moment had arrived, she felt a flutter of anxiety. What if nobody showed up? What if all her work—all those sleepless nights of planning and prepping—led to an absolutely empty room?

Just as the thought crossed her mind, the door jingled beside her, startling her from her musing. Shelby stepped through with Lacy close behind.

"There she is, the lady of the hour!" Shelby said, a broad smile on her face as she pulled Cami into a hug.

"You made it!" Cami said, her shoulders relaxing a little. "I was starting to worry that nobody would show up."

"Are you kidding? This place looks amazing,"

Lacy said, looking around the studio. "Besides, we're ten minutes early. You really transformed the space. It's beautiful, Cami."

"Thank you. I wanted it to feel festive but not too over the top or tacky. I mean, it is a yoga studio, not Santa's workshop."

Lacy laughed. "You nailed it. It's perfect."

Shelby handed Cami a small potted poinsettia wrapped in a festive red bow. "A little gift for you. It's not much, but I thought it might bring more Christmas cheer to your space."

"Thank you. It's perfect. I'll put it right by the tree."

As Cami arranged the poinsettia near the small Christmas tree in the corner, more guests started trickling in from the sidewalk outside. Friends from the neighborhood, yoga students she had taught at other locations, and a few curious locals made their way in. She could hear the soft chatter and laughter as people filed in. Her nerves slowly gave way to excitement. This was it. Her dream was coming to life.

"I told you people would come," Lacy said, nudging her gently as she handed her a cup of peppermint tea. "You're going to do great things here."

Cami smiled. "I hope so. I want this to be a place where people feel comfortable and empowered, where they can come and breathe and meditate, you know."

Shelby nodded. "Well, you've done that. It's a calming space, and it's got your positive energy all over it. People are going to love coming here."

"I could live here," Lacy said with a grin. "This place is a dream."

"I know, right? It's very relaxing," Shelby said, laughing.

Cami had set up a small seating area with cozy floor cushions and blankets. A group of women had already gathered, sipping tea and discussing their holiday plans. Cami was thrilled that the open house was going so well. For a long time, she had thought any chance at a better life after her ex-husband went back to prison was out of reach. But now she knew she could have a second chance to make her life exactly what she wanted it to be.

CHAPTER 7

SHELBY STOOD behind the counter at *Tattered Pages*, the independent bookstore where she worked. She could hear the gentle hum of Christmas music filling the space, and the freshly brewed coffee in the café drew her in. The late afternoon light filtered through the windows, lighting up her favorite things —lines of bookshelves. It was a slow day, which she didn't mind. She loved having time to organize displays and read the new books that came in.

A giant Christmas tree decorated with tiny book-themed ornaments and red bows stood near the entrance. She smiled as she walked over and adjusted one of them. Just then, the bell above the door jingled, and she looked up to see Lacy walking in with her arms full of shopping bags. Her usual composed expression looked a little strained, and her smile was a bit forced as she approached the counter.

"Well, well, well," Shelby said. "It looks like you've been busy doing some Christmas shopping."

Lacy nodded, setting her bags down with a loud sigh. "Yeah, I figured I'd get it all done in one go if I could, but this is exhausting. I've done an awful lot of online shopping this year." She looked around the store and smiled. "It's much more peaceful in here than out there. I needed this."

"Well, you're welcome to escape here, always," Shelby said, walking over and pouring her a cup of coffee from the pot. "Take a load off. You look like you need a break."

Lacy gratefully accepted the coffee and sat on one of the stools near the counter. She ran her fingers through her blonde hair, which had come loose from the ponytail she'd tied it in earlier. "Shopping for the kids always seems so simple in my mind, but then I get out here and get overwhelmed with all the options. Don't even get me started on the crowds out there."

"I understand," Shelby said, shaking her head. "I'm not a fan of the crowds either. I love online shopping, maybe a little too much."

Lacy laughed softly but then went quiet. Her eyes drifted around the room to the holiday decorations as she sipped her coffee. Shelby noticed a shift in her mood, the way her shoulders seemed tense, and a distant look in her eyes.

"Hey, Lacy," she said gently, leaning forward. "What's going on with you?"

Lacy looked up, blinking as if she hadn't realized just how lost in thought she'd been. She opened her mouth but then sighed, putting her cup down. "It's just... it's something I can't talk about, or at least I'm not supposed to."

Shelby was growing a little concerned. What secret was Lacy keeping that had her tied up in knots like this? Her last secret had caused so much drama in her life, and she didn't want to see her friend go through that again. For a moment, Shelby considered the possibilities. Maybe she'd gotten back with her ex-husband. Maybe one of her kids was sick. Or she was ill. Shelby felt her stomach tying itself in knots.

"Look, I know this is something you feel like you can't tell anybody, but I just want you to know that you can tell me anything. It won't go any further."

Lacy looked at her as if she was trying to decide whether to share her confidence. She sighed. "My

RACHEL HANNA

agent called me the other day and told me that some producers are interested in making one of my books into a movie." She said it so fast, as if she was trying to chase the words right out of her mouth.

Shelby's jaw dropped. "Oh my gosh, Lacy, that's wonderful. Congratulations!"

Lacy held up her hand. "See, that's why I don't want to tell anybody. Do you know how embarrassing it would be if this thing doesn't go through? Everybody will be looking at me and gossiping about me."

"Your friends would never do that," Shelby said.

"Willadeene would."

Shelby rolled her eyes and laughed. "Well, I don't know that we can necessarily count her as a friend. She's more of a crazy adopted grandmother type."

Lacy chuckled, her shoulders finally dropping from her ears. "It's just that when my agent told me that, I started to get stressed out. Instead of being excited, I feel pressured."

"Why do you think that is?" Shelby asked.

"I guess because if it doesn't happen, I will feel like a failure."

"But you're not a failure. You've done well in your author career."

"I know that, and I'm proud of everything I've

done so far. But if they decline to sign an option, I will feel like something was taken away from me."

"Look, most people don't get this opportunity, Lacy. This is a dream for an author. Just the fact that you've even been considered is proof that you touch people's lives with your books. That you don't just entertain them, but you make them feel something. I'm sure whether it's now or in the future, somebody is going to want to make your books into a movie."

"You think so?" Lacy asked, scrunching her nose a bit.

Shelby reached over and squeezed her hand. "Of course I do. And now that you've told me, you can share all the big news with me, and I swear I won't tell a soul."

"I trust you," Lacy said, taking a sip of her coffee.

"So when do you think you'll hear something?"

Lacy traced the rim of the cup with her finger. "I don't know. It's just been a few days. This whole thing is a very long process from what I understand. First, you have to get them interested, and then you sign an option. Most of the time, nothing ever happens after that. The options expire, and no movies or TV shows are made."

"You're in limbo; understandably, that's making

you a little anxious. But don't be worried. This is just icing on the cake. And you already have a huge cake."

Lacy smiled. "Thanks, Shelby. You always know how to make me feel better. How are you doing?"

"Well, I'm a little worried about the whole wedding thing, of course."

"And you know that you can trust me," Lacy said. "You know I'm going to make sure your wedding is amazing."

"I know, it's just not what I imagined, and I'm having a hard time getting excited about walking out of my kitchen into the backyard to get married."

"Well, we're not exactly having a barbecue," Lacy said, waving her hand. "It's going to be great. You just have to trust that I will get this right. I'll make sure that you have the wedding of your dreams."

Shelby forced a smile. "I know you're going to do everything you can, and I know that all that really matters at the end of the day is that I'm Reed's wife. But I had a cruddy first marriage, and I want this to be something I can look back on for the rest of my life."

Lacy grabbed both of her hands. "This day will be your very best memory, I promise."

Willadeene stood in her small, cluttered kitchen, washing the last of her breakfast dishes. As the water splashed against the plates, she scrubbed aggressively. It had been a quiet day, unusually so. She did not enjoy silence. She preferred to keep herself busy, whether it was working in her garden, tending to her collection of dying houseplants, or looking out at the neighborhood from her window. She didn't like to sit around and do nothing, even at her age.

"Stupid crumbs," she muttered to herself, scrubbing a stubborn spot of toast from the plate. The sun streamed through the windows as she dried her hands on a dish towel and then looked at the clock.

"Mail should be here soon," she said, talking to herself. It was common for her to talk to herself. After all, she had nobody else to talk to. Her daily routine of checking the mail was something she looked forward to. She knew that was pretty sad, but it was what it was. It gave her a sense of structure in a life that sometimes felt like it had lost its purpose.

She hung the dish towel on a hook, pulled on her jacket, and walked outside. The air was crisp, a rare cool day for Charleston in late November. As she stepped out onto her front porch, her eyes narrowed when she saw a car she didn't recognize pull up at the end of her driveway. She squinted, trying to make out the figure getting out of the car.

And then her heart jolted at the sight of the unmistakable form of her sister, Gertie.

"What in good gracious…" Willadeene whispered under her breath. Her entire body tensed up, and she stood there, frozen in place, as she watched Gertie slowly make her way toward the house and the Uber drive away. She looked much older than she remembered, her hair grayer and her movements slower. Same as Willadeene.

The sight of her sister stirred up old, deep wounds and an anger that Willadeene thought she had buried a long time ago. She marched off the porch, hands on her hips, balled into fists at her sides.

"What on earth do you think you're doing here?" she demanded, her voice as unwelcoming as possible.

Gertie stopped at the foot of the front porch steps, looking up at her. "Willadeene, I just want to talk."

"Talk?" Willadeene barked back with a laugh. "We haven't talked in over thirty years, Gertie, and now you just show up at my house like nothing happened? You sure have some nerve."

"I know," Gertie said, her voice soft. "I know it's been a long time. It's been too long. But I—"

"Save it," Willadeene snapped, cutting her off and holding her hand up. She crossed her arms and glared at her. "You should have stayed wherever you've been all these years. Go crawl back under that rock. I don't need you showing up here now, acting like you care."

Gertie stood there, her shoulders slumping. "But I do care. I've been trying to reach you, Willadeene. I wrote letters."

"Yeah, I got your letters," Willadeene said coldly. "I read every one of them, and then I tossed them in the trash where they belong."

Gertie flinched at the harshness of her words, but she still didn't move. "Please just give me a chance to explain, to make amends."

"No," Willadeene said firmly. "I don't need any explanations from you. Not after what you did."

Gertie stepped forward slightly, her eyes pleading. "I know I hurt you and have regretted it every day since then, but we're sisters, Willadeene. We're all that we have left of our family, and we were close once. I just want to make things right. Can't we try?"

Willadeene held up her hand again, her face hard like stone. "You don't get to come waltzing back into my life like nothing ever happened, and you don't get to decide when it's time to 'make things right,'" she said, using air quotes. "You screwed me over, and then you weren't even here when I needed you. I was always there when you needed me."

Gertie opened her mouth to speak, but Willadeene's anger only grew as memories flooded back. Things that she had pushed away were bursting through her mind. She stepped closer.

"When I lost my husband, you didn't even call. Not once. You left me to pick up the pieces of my life all by myself, and now, after all this time, you think you can just show up here and fix everything with a few empty words? Well, I've got news for you, Gertie. There's no fixing this."

Tears filled Gertie's eyes, but they didn't move Willadeene. She had learned how to harden herself over the years. She had seen plenty of Gertie's tears in her life, and they wouldn't affect her now.

"I'm not asking for forgiveness," Gertie whispered. "I know I can't undo what I did, but I've missed you, Willadeene. I've missed having my sister."

Her chest tightened at the word *sister*, but she quickly pushed the emotions aside. "We stopped being sisters a long time ago. You made sure of that."

Gertie pulled out a piece of paper from her pocket. "I don't expect you to forgive me, but I want to give you this."

Willadeene's eyes narrowed. "What is that?"

"Just read it when you're ready," Gertie said.

Willadeene stared at the paper for a long moment before snatching it out of her hand. She crumpled it in her fist without even looking at it. "I don't need anything from you. Not letters, not explanations, and not apologies."

"Willadeene, I'll go. I'm sorry, but if you ever do want to talk—"

"I don't," Willadeene snapped. "And don't you come back here. You're not welcome."

With that, she turned on her heel and marched back toward her house. She could feel Gertie's eyes following her, but she didn't look back. She slammed the door behind her, the sound echoing through her quiet, lonely home. Her heart pounded in her chest, which wasn't something that happened regularly, given that she was on heart medication that typically kept her heart rate slow.

She looked at the crumpled piece of paper in her hand. She thought about throwing it straight into the trash, but something stopped her. She stuffed it in the side table—out of sight, out of mind—and then moved back to the kitchen. She just couldn't shake the feeling that Gertie's visit had unsettled something deep within her that she wasn't quite ready to face.

Shelby sat cross-legged on the plush rug in the children's section of *Tattered Pages*, surrounded by a group of wide-eyed children. The soft glow of the Christmas tree behind her twinkled in the background. In her lap was a brightly illustrated book called *Pip's First Christmas*. It was a heartwarming story about a young penguin celebrating his first Christmas with his new adoptive family.

"And so," Shelby said to the children, "Pip the penguin looked around the cozy igloo filled with twinkling lights and decorations. For the first time, he felt something fluttering in his heart. It wasn't just the cold of the snow or the excitement of the new gifts. It was love—the love of a family who wanted him just as he was."

The children sat in rapt attention, their little hands resting on their laps.

"This," Pip said, snuggling close to his new family, "is the best Christmas ever."

Shelby smiled as she closed the book. She held up the cover for the children to see the final illustration of the cute little penguin wearing a red scarf, surrounded by his new family. The kids clapped, some of them bouncing up and down.

"Again, again!" one of the little girls cried out.

Shelby laughed softly. "We'll have to save the next one for next week's reading hour," she said. "But don't forget, you can check out books to read at home with your parents, too."

The bookstore had a small children's section where books could be checked out, just like at the library. It was mostly stocked with returned or donated books. The children started to gather around the bookshelf to pick out their favorite stories as Shelby stood up, brushing her hands down the front of her Christmas sweater. It was her favorite, a festive green color with a line of reindeer prancing across the middle.

She put the book back on the shelf when she caught sight of Reed standing by the door, leaning casually against the frame with his arms crossed, a warm smile on his face.

"Hey, you," Shelby said, her heart fluttering at the sight of him.

"Hey, yourself," he said, walking over to her. "I

didn't want to interrupt the story. Looked like you had a very captivated audience."

She smiled, looking over at the kids as most of them ran to their parents, books clutched in their tiny little hands. "This is one of my favorite things to do here—read books to the kids, especially Christmas stories. This one's about a little penguin who gets adopted."

He nodded, his hand finding the small of her back as they watched the last of the kids leave. The soft hum of Christmas music filled the background, and the bookstore felt incredibly cozy today—especially now that Reed was here.

"You're amazing with them," he said after a moment. "I can see how much you love this."

She turned to face him fully. "I do love it. I've always dreamed of being surrounded by kids, especially during the holidays."

His eyes searched hers for a brief moment. She could feel the weight of unspoken thoughts between them. He tucked a loose strand of hair behind her ear.

"You know, I've been thinking," he said. "About us and our future. I know we've talked about it, but I want you to know that if we want to have a family, I'm all in—whatever that looks like for us."

She swallowed the lump in her throat. The idea of her own family was something she had dreamed about since she was a little girl. But when she realized she couldn't have kids, it seemed like the end had come before she even had a chance to try.

"I've always wanted to adopt," she said. "Even before I knew I couldn't have kids of my own, it's something that's been on my heart for a long time."

He cupped her chin in his hand. "Then we'll adopt," he said. "There are so many kids out there who need love, who need a home, and we can be that for them."

"You really mean that?"

"Of course I do," he said. "I love you, Shelby. I want to build a life with you—a family. And however that happens, I'm ready for it."

She leaned into him, resting her head against his chest as he wrapped his arms around her. She closed her eyes, feeling the steady beat of his heart beneath her cheek.

"I've been scared that I won't be able to have kids, won't be able to have my own family, and I thought maybe that wouldn't be enough for you."

He pulled back just enough to tilt her chin up. "Shelby, you're more than enough all by yourself. You always have been, and you always will be. And if adopting is what you've always wanted, then that's what we'll do—together."

"Okay," she finally said. "But if we're adopting, I need you to know that I'll probably want more than one."

He laughed, kissing the top of her head. "Deal, but let's start with one, okay? Let's not go looking for triplets on our first go," he joked.

Maybe by next Christmas, they'd have an extra stocking hanging on the mantle, Shelby thought. At least a girl could dream.

CHAPTER 8

Reed walked back and forth in his office with his cell phone in his hand, his fingers tapping against the side of his desk. He glanced at the clock to check the time. This call was very important, and he wanted to make sure everything went perfectly. He'd spent days planning this idea, and now it was finally coming together, but Shelby couldn't know — not yet.

When the phone finally connected, his voice was calm but firm. "Hey, this is Reed Sullivan. I'm just calling to confirm the details we discussed for the setup," he said. He kept his tone professional, although his heart was racing with excitement about what Shelby would think of this idea.

The voice on the other end greeted him warmly.

Reed pressed the speaker button so he didn't have to hold the phone to his ear.

"Yes, Mr. Sullivan, we've got everything you sent over. We'll be able to deliver exactly as planned. Remind me again how soon you need it."

Reed looked out his office window. His and Shelby's wedding was only a couple of weeks away, and though she had her own vision for how things would go, not everything had gone according to plan. But this — this was going to be the surprise of a lifetime.

"Our wedding is on Christmas Eve. It will be hard to get this past my fiancée since we're getting married in her backyard. Is that going to work for you?"

There was a brief pause on the other end.

"Yes, I think we can make it work, but is there a possibility you could get her away from the house the day before for a little while? It'll take us a couple of hours to get things set up, and then you'll need to keep her away until you're ready for her to see the surprise."

Reed took a deep breath and blew it out slowly. "I think I can do it. I've got some friends who'll be willing to help me." He smiled to himself, imagining the look on Shelby's face when she saw what he had planned. "It's a small gathering, nothing too chaotic, but I just want everything to be perfect, as you can imagine. No hiccups."

The woman on the other end of the phone chuckled. "You can count on us. This kind of project is a challenge, but we love working on unique requests and making wedding days perfect."

A sense of relief washed over Reed. "Great. And to confirm, this is going to be the real deal. Nothing fake. I don't want anything half-done."

"Absolutely," she replied. "It's going to be exactly what you envisioned. We're going to create the perfect atmosphere."

His eyes gleamed with excitement as he leaned against the window frame. "Perfect. This will mean a lot to my fiancée, so I appreciate your efforts."

"We understand. It's a big moment, and we'll make sure it's unforgettable."

"Unforgettable," he echoed, a smile tugging at the corner of his lips. "That's exactly what I'm looking for."

After finalizing a few more details and confirming the time for setup, Reed ended the call and sat down in his chair, running his fingers through his hair. He couldn't wait to see Shelby's reaction when it all came together. This was going to be a dream come true.

Leaning back in his chair, excitement bubbled up inside him. This would be a Christmas neither of them would ever forget, and it was just the beginning of their life together.

Shelby stood in her kitchen, humming along with the Christmas music that she had softly playing in the background. She had gingerbread cookies baking in the oven, which caused a beautiful smell to linger in the air. Willadeene had stopped by her house earlier, full of her normal complaints, but Shelby didn't mind. Willadeene had become a constant presence in her life, and she'd grown oddly fond of her despite her prickly personality.

She maneuvered around the kitchen, wiping down countertops and just enjoying some time alone in her home. She loved Christmas. She loved the smell of the candles she had around the bottom floor. She loved her Christmas tree lit up all day long. She loved her hearth and the garland she had draped across it. Christmas was the one time of year when she thought everyone should feel peaceful and joyful.

Of course, she also felt stressed out. Her wedding was only a couple of weeks away, and she still didn't know how they would get everything done and have it in her backyard. But today, she was trying not to think about it. Today was a stress-free day. She was gifting that to herself.

As she was lost in thought, planning out the next few days, a sudden knock at her front door startled her. She glanced at the clock. It was way past time for usual visitors, and she wasn't expecting anyone. She wiped her hands on a Christmas-themed dish towel and walked toward the front door.

When she opened it, she was a little bit speechless. A woman was standing on her porch. She was older, her shoulders hunched forward, her hands clutching a small purse tightly in front of her. She had silver-gray hair that framed her face, but her face was etched with worry. Her eyes almost looked like they had a quiet desperation. And she looked like Willadeene. That was unmistakable.

"I'm sorry to just show up like this," the woman said softly, her voice quivering. "But do you know Willadeene?"

Shelby blinked, trying to process what was

happening. "Yes, I do. Very well, actually. And you are?"

"I'm Gertie," the woman said, swallowing hard. "I'm Willadeene's sister."

Shelby's heart dropped. Gertie. That sister that Willadeene had refused to speak about, except in bitter, clipped sentences. The estranged sister who had been absent from Willadeene's life for more than thirty years. Shelby had never expected this visit. Not at all.

"Please come in," Shelby said, stepping aside. She momentarily peeked out the door to make sure that Willadeene wasn't seeing this play out in front of her.

Gertie walked into the living room and sat down, her eyes darting around as if she wasn't sure that was the right thing to do. "I'm so sorry to drop by like this unannounced. I know it's terribly rude," she said, wringing her hands. "But I just don't know where else to go."

Shelby closed the front door and walked over, sitting down across from Gertie. This was the woman that Willadeene had made out to be some awful person, but she looked fairly nice. Of course, looks could be deceiving. "What exactly is going on?" Shelby asked. "Why are you here?"

Gertie hesitated, her fingers gripping her purse so tightly that her knuckles were turning white. "I tried to talk to Willadeene," she said. "I wrote her letters first, of course, and tried to call her, but she wouldn't respond, so I showed up at her house."

Shelby's nose scrunched. "And I bet that didn't go very well."

"No, it didn't go very well, not at all," Gertie said. There was a pain in her eyes, and Shelby knew how stubborn Willadeene could be.

"I know it's hard, but maybe this is something that just can't be fixed."

Gertie shook her head. "Our mother always taught us that everything could be fixed if you just said you were sorry and showed that you had changed. I've been trying to do that with Willadeene. I've been trying to make amends, and she won't even let me get a full sentence out before she kicks me off her property. I need more time."

"I understand," Shelby said, "but I'm not sure how I can help you."

"I did hurt her. I made some mistakes. But we're the only two members of our family left, and we're not getting any younger. I can't just let it end like this."

"I wish I knew what to say. Willadeene is a bit

difficult, as you know, and I don't think she's ready to forgive and forget."

Gertie nodded, her eyes welling with tears. "I don't expect her to forgive me right away. I just wanted a chance to talk to her, to explain. I've missed her so much over the years, and I don't want to live the rest of my life without at least trying to make things right."

Shelby's heart ached for the older woman. She couldn't completely understand what she was going through, but she could imagine how hard it would be to reach an older age and desperately try to make up with your family member who wasn't interested. It was obvious that Gertie wanted to reconcile.

"What do you need from me?" Shelby asked.

"I don't have anywhere else to go. The hotels are all booked for the holidays, and I don't want to leave Charleston and go back to Florida without trying to talk to Willadeene. Would it be too much to ask if I could just stay here for a few nights, just until I can figure out what to do next?"

Shelby's heart sank. She couldn't let Gertie stay at her house right under Willadeene's nose. She was stepping out into the middle of a minefield.

"I don't think that's a good idea," Shelby said slowly. "Willadeene is very set in her ways, and she's already told me and you that she doesn't want to reconnect. Sometimes, it might just be better to cut your losses."

"I'll stay out of her way," Gertie said quickly. "I won't be any trouble, I promise. I just need a place to stay until I can figure this out. I don't have anywhere else to go."

Shelby stared at Gertie, feeling the weight of her plea. She could see how broken and desperate she was. But Shelby knew this wouldn't be an easy fix, and she didn't want to be caught between two sisters while also trying to plan her wedding. But how could she turn the older woman away? With Christmas right around the corner and nowhere for her to go, that didn't seem very kind.

"Okay," Shelby said finally, letting out a sigh. "You can stay in the guest room upstairs, and I'll try to talk to Willadeene for you. I can't promise anything, but maybe she'll at least hear you out."

"Oh, thank you, thank you so much. You don't know what this means to me," Gertie said, leaning over and squeezing Shelby's hand.

"We need to just take it one step at a time. But you have to stay hidden. You can't let Willadeene see that you're here."

"Of course. I will be quiet as a mouse," Gertie said.

Shelby stood up and walked toward the stairs, with Gertie following behind her. They passed the Christmas tree, and for a moment, Shelby thought about how peaceful everything had been just a few moments ago. But now she would be a mediator between two stubborn sisters right before her wedding. This wasn't exactly how she thought things were going to go.

Shelby got to her favorite local cafe just as Willadeene was walking up. Joan had brought Willadeene into town to do a little shopping just to get her out of the house and was dropping her off with Shelby to take her back home since she had more things to do. It was okay because Shelby needed to talk to Willadeene. Having Gertie living in her house for the last twenty-four hours was starting to freak her out. Willadeene often dropped by unannounced, and the last thing she needed was for her to see her estranged sister sitting in Shelby's living room.

Gertie had been good about staying upstairs. Last

night, Shelby told her to come down and get dinner, and she just about had to force her.

Willadeene shuffled toward the entrance, her purse clutched tightly in her hand. She was wearing her regular irritated expression. Shelby was struck by just how much the sisters looked alike. Willadeene held her purse just like Gertie did at the front door. But Gertie was soft-spoken and kind, while Willadeene was... Well, she was Willadeene.

"Hey, Willadeene," Shelby called out, waving from across the cafe.

Willadeene looked at her but didn't break the rigid lines of her features.

"Well, you're early," she said to Shelby.

"I know. I made sure to get here on time." Shelby tended to be a little late, and Willadeene hated it.

Willadeene sat down across from her in the booth, sliding into the seat without even looking at the menu.

"So, what are you going to have today?" Shelby asked. She knew what Willadeene was going to have. They'd eaten here before several times. Willadeene was a creature of habit.

"The meatloaf special, of course. You know it's the only thing worth eating here," Willadeene said with a huff, sliding the laminated menu across the table.

After they ordered, Shelby folded her hands on the table, watching Willadeene fiddle with her napkin.

"So, how have you been today?" Shelby asked.

Willadeene grunted, shrugging her shoulders. "Same old, same old. Nothing in my life changes except the weather, and even that can't make up its mind."

Shelby took a deep breath. She needed to dive into this before she lost her nerve.

"I've been meaning to talk to you about something, Willadeene."

"Talk about what?" Willadeene's eyes narrowed.

"It's about your sister, Gertie."

At the mention of her sister's name, Willadeene's entire body stiffened. Her lips pressed into an even thinner line, and her eyes darkened. It was something that looked like a mixture of pain and anger.

"I have nothing to say about her," Willadeene snapped. She grabbed a sugar packet on the table and crumpled it in her hand.

"I know," Shelby said, trying to be gentle, "but I think you should. You know she's been reaching out to you. You said she wrote letters. She's called."

"And let me stop you right there," Willadeene said, holding up her hand. "I don't care what she's done. It's too late. You don't know what she's put me through."

Shelby sighed. "I know she hurt you, but it's been over three decades, and she's your sister. Don't you think it's time to let some of that go?"

Willadeene leaned back against the booth, crossing her arms. "Forgiveness is overrated. People act like just saying 'I'm sorry' fixes things. But you know what? It doesn't, not after what she did. She ignored me when I needed her most, and now she wants to come crawling back? No. She made her choices."

Shelby frowned. She'd known Willadeene for well over a year now, and she could be difficult. But she always had sensed that beneath that tough exterior was a woman who had been hurt and used anger as a shield.

"She's been trying, Willadeene. You said she came all the way to Charleston to see you. Don't you think that means something?"

"No. It doesn't mean anything," Willadeene said flatly. "She was only here because she's an old woman who feels guilty. And you know what? She should. I don't need her pity."

Shelby leaned forward. "I'm not asking you to forgive her overnight, but maybe you could at least hear her out. Let her explain."

Willadeene scoffed. "Explanations are worthless to me. What I need is to be left alone. I'm too old to be dealing with all this nonsense."

Their food arrived, the plates clattering onto the table, but neither of them reached for their forks. Shelby leaned back. She had tried. But Willadeene was as stubborn as ever, and it seemed that nothing she said would change her mind.

"I don't want you to regret not giving your sister a chance. You're both getting older, and family is very important. Especially around the holidays."

Willadeene's eyes flickered with something that Shelby couldn't quite place. But then she replaced it quickly with her hard expression.

"Family?" Willadeene said under her breath, stabbing at the meatloaf with her fork. "Yeah, some great family I have."

CHAPTER 9

SHELBY'S MIND was still spinning around after her conversation with Willadeene. Getting through to her was like trying to bang your head through a brick wall. It was painful, and it didn't lead anywhere. She felt very deflated. She had hoped that Willadeene might soften a little, but whatever her wounds were, they ran a lot deeper than Shelby had first realized.

After dropping Willadeene off in her driveway and watching her go inside, Shelby pulled into her own driveway, stepped out of her car, and was startled to see Gertie standing there at her front door, her hands shoved in the pockets of her coat. It wasn't exactly cold outside, but she was older, so maybe she was sensitive to any cold. Her face was pinched with worry, and Shelby's heart sank. Gertie was here, no doubt hoping for good news, but she wasn't about to get it.

"Gertie," Shelby called out as she walked towards her porch. "What are you doing out here?"

Gertie turned to look at her. Her eyes were wide with hope.

"I was just hoping you had a chance to talk to Willadeene. I saw her leave this morning, so I thought maybe…"

Shelby paused, feeling a lump forming in her throat. "Actually, I did talk to her, Gertie. I tried, but…" She shook her head. The hope drained from Gertie's face. "She's just not ready, and honestly, I'm not sure if she'll ever be."

Gertie's shoulders slumped, her face obviously disappointed. "She still won't see or talk to me."

Shelby sighed and walked up the steps, placing a hand on Gertie's arm. "I'm so sorry. She's just holding on to a lot of hurt, and I don't understand exactly what happened between you two, but she's just not willing to do anything to mend fences right now."

Gertie's eyes filled with tears. She looked away, her voice barely above a whisper. "I don't know what else to do. I've tried everything. I don't want to leave here without trying to fix things, but the truth is I have nowhere else to go. It's either here or drive all the way back to Florida. The hotels are all booked for the holidays, and I just don't have anyone else here that I know. Willadeene's obviously not going to let me stay with her."

Shelby felt her heart squeeze. She had no idea that the situation was this dire, and all she could think about was her own mother. What if she was in a situation like this and she needed help? The idea of turning Gertie away right before Christmas left a very bitter taste in her mouth.

"I know this is something big to ask," Gertie said, her voice trembling, "but is there a way I could keep staying with you just for a few more nights until I figure out what I'm going to do? I'll stay out of the way. I won't cause any trouble, I promise."

Shelby hesitated. She felt the weight of the decision pressing down on her like a concrete block. She knew just how furious Willadeene would be if she found out Gertie was staying with her, but Gertie was desperate, and how was Shelby going to turn her away? She thought for a long moment and then nodded.

"I guess that's okay, but we have to keep this our

secret. Willadeene would literally push me down a flight of stairs if she found out. I shouldn't be getting involved like this, Gertie."

Tears of gratitude filled Gertie's eyes, and she reached out to grab Shelby's hands. "Thank you so much. I can't tell you how much this means to me, and I won't be a problem, and if you need me to do anything, I'm glad to do it. Clean the bathroom or make dinner."

Shelby chuckled and offered a weak smile. "That's not what guests need to do. You're welcome to stay. Consider it my Christmas gift to you."

"I'm so thankful, Shelby. I just have to make things right with my sister."

Shelby stood in front of her stove, stirring a pot of spaghetti sauce. Her mind was racing. Reed was going to be here any minute, and she hadn't figured out how to tell him what she had done, that during the middle of stressful last-minute wedding preparations, she had somehow gotten herself into this mess, and now Gertie was upstairs napping in her guest room. She meant well doing what she did, but the weight of the choice was hitting her now that she was downstairs alone, standing in front of her pot of spaghetti sauce.

She looked at the clock on the wall. It was approaching 7 p.m., and she knew that Reed would be walking through the door any moment. She wasn't sure how he would react to this news, but she had a feeling he wouldn't be thrilled about it.

Just as she was lost in her thoughts, she heard the front door open, and Reed stepped inside. She turned to see him walking into the kitchen with a bottle of wine, a warm smile on his face.

"Hey, sweetie," he greeted, coming up and kissing her on the cheek. "Something smells amazing in here."

She forced a smile. "Hey yourself," she said, trying to keep her tone light. "Making spaghetti. I'm sure it's not as good as what you make at the restaurant, but it'll suffice."

He laughed. "It smells delicious, and I'm sure it will be wonderful. What's wrong? You seem off," he said, his brows furrowing.

She put down the wooden spoon she had been holding. "I need to tell you something."

His smile faded. "Okay, what's going on? Is this about the wedding?"

She bit her lip and shook her head. "No, the

wedding's fine. It's just that I have a house guest upstairs."

He looked up at the ceiling and then back at her. "A house guest? What do you mean?"

"I told Gertie that she could stay here. Well, *hide* here, more like it."

He blinked, his expression changing to confusion. "Gertie? You mean Willadeene's sister?"

She nodded, feeling a new wave of anxiety wash over her. "Yep, the very same one. She showed up here the other day, begging for a place to stay so she could keep trying to fix things with Willadeene. She said she didn't have anywhere else to go. It's the holidays, and the hotels are all booked. So it was either have her drive all the way back to Florida right before Christmas or let her stay here until she could make things right with Willadeene. So she's in the guest room, at least for a few nights."

His eyes widened. He let out a slow breath and then ran his fingers through his hair. "Shelby, do you realize what you've gotten yourself into?"

"I know, I know," she said, holding up her hands. "It's complicated, and I know Willadeene will be upset if she ever finds out. But Gertie just seemed so desperate, and it made me think of my mother. I couldn't turn her away. It's Christmas, Reed."

He leaned against the counter. "So you're in the middle of a family feud that's been going on for decades, right before our wedding. Do you really think you can fix this without losing your mind?"

She heard doubt in his voice, which made her heart sink because he was right. She had no business messing around with this. "I know it's a big mess, but they're sisters. They've just been estranged for so long. I think maybe if they had a little help, they could find their way back to each other."

He crossed his arms. "And so you think sneaking Gertie into your house without telling Willadeene will help?"

"Well, I was going to talk to Willadeene. I mean, I already tried, but she's so closed off. She won't even listen to the idea of sitting down and talking to her sister."

"But again, you think hiding Gertie here is the answer?" His voice was gentle but firm. "If Willadeene finds out on her own, she will feel so betrayed."

"I know," Shelby said, rubbing her hands over her face, "but what would you have done? I mean, Gertie is staying here to try to make things right. She just wants a chance to talk, and Willadeene is so dang stubborn. I thought if I could get her to soften up a little bit, she might at least hear her out."

"You know, Willadeene's not like softening up a stick of butter, Shelby. She's more like trying to soften up a concrete block."

Shelby laughed. "Not funny."

Reed walked over to her, placing his hands on her shoulders. "I get it. I really do. You're a kind person. You have the biggest heart of anybody I know, and I love that about you. But this is a very delicate situation. You're trying to play matchmaker with two women who haven't spoken to each other in many years. It won't be as simple as just getting them in the same room."

"But they're getting older, Reed. They don't have a lot of time left to fix these things. What if I'm the only person who can help them reconnect? I don't want Willadeene to regret never giving her sister a chance, and I don't want Gertie to go back to Florida without at least some closure."

He searched her face for a long moment. "I know you mean well, but I think you should tell Willadeene. She deserves to know that Gertie's here."

Her heart raced at the thought. "She'd be furious. She might never talk to me again."

He smiled faintly, brushing a loose strand of hair behind her ear. "You can't get rid of Willadeene that easily. Besides, you're trying to help. She needs to know her sister is staying with you. What if something goes wrong and she sees her?"

"I don't know. I'm just trying to do the right thing."

"Well, you can't fix everything for everyone."

She leaned into him and pressed her cheek against his chest as he put his arms around her. "I'm a romantic at heart, you know," she said quietly. "I just want them to find their way back to each other. They were close once, and I think they could be again."

He kissed the top of her head. "I know you want that. Your optimism is one of the things I love most about you, but sometimes even romantics have to let people find their own way."

"I'll think about talking to Willadeene, telling her that Gertie's here, but I'm not sure that's the best way to go."

"You'll figure out the right thing to do. You always do."

"Well, I'm glad you believe in me because right now, I think I've made one of the worst decisions of my life."

Shelby's house was filled with the scent of popcorn as the fireplace crackled and the festive decorations shimmered in the light. She stood at the kitchen counter, carefully putting the large bowl of popcorn in the center of a tray next to mugs of hot chocolate topped with whipped cream and candy canes.

This was her favorite time of year, especially since she was getting married on Christmas Eve. Now, it would be her favorite time of year for two reasons. She loved the twinkling Christmas lights, the scent of pine from the candle on her kitchen table, and the sense of togetherness that always seemed to settle over the holidays. She knew not everyone was as fortunate as she was, and she didn't take that for granted.

Reed was in the living room adjusting the volume on the TV with the opening credits for the movie *Elf* scrolling across the screen. Lacy was on the couch, snuggled under a fluffy red blanket with her legs tucked beneath her. Cami was lounging next to her, scrolling through her phone while she bit off the arms of a gingerbread cookie.

"Movie night is officially starting in five minutes," Shelby yelled from the kitchen. She balanced the tray in her hands as she maneuvered around the counter.

"Finally," Lacy said, "I've been looking forward to this all week. I need some good holiday laughs."

Cami nodded. "Yeah, after the craziness of starting the yoga studio and running around for some last-minute shopping, I needed this too. You've really outdone yourself with the decorations and the food."

Shelby beamed as she set the tray down on the coffee table. The garland draped across the fireplace mantel had two stockings hanging beneath it, one for her and one for Reed, although she wasn't expecting Santa to fill them.

"Thanks," she said. She settled into the chair beside Reed, who slipped an arm around her shoulders. "I wanted it to feel extra festive this year."

"Well, you nailed it," Lacy said, grabbing a mug of hot chocolate as she sank further into the couch. "This is the perfect setting for movie night. I wish Joan could have come."

"Yeah, I know, but she had a date, and we don't want to interfere with that," Shelby said, laughing.

"Okay," Reed announced, holding the remote up, "who's ready to watch *Elf* for the fifteenth time?"

"I am!" Shelby said, raising her hand. "It's a

Christmas tradition. You can't have a Christmas movie night without *Elf*."

Reed smirked. "Okay, okay, let's get it going."

As the movie started, the room settled into a comfortable rhythm. The familiar sounds of the movie filled the air, and soon, they were all laughing at the same scenes each had watched year after year. But there was something special about watching these kinds of movies together, surrounded by friends.

"Oh my gosh, this is my favorite part," Cami said, leaning forward as the character gulped down a bottle of maple syrup.

"How does he do that without getting sick?" Lacy asked, shaking her head. "I would be in a sugar coma after one sip."

"I guess it's one of life's greatest mysteries," Shelby said, laughing.

They bantered back and forth, with Reed telling them to be quiet repeatedly. The sound of popcorn crunching in the warmth of the fireplace made everyone feel perfectly at ease. They didn't really need the fireplace going; it was Charleston, after all, but tonight, it had dipped down into the high forties, and they figured they could get away with it for one night.

Shelby leaned into Reed's side, feeling content and thankful for this life she had created here. Even in the middle of wedding planning stress and the drama of the Willadeene and Gertie saga, moments like this reminded her of the importance of friendship. She had invited Gertie to come downstairs if she wanted, but she didn't want to take any chances. Willadeene could show up without warning.

And in true Willadeene fashion, halfway through *Elf*, she suddenly walked through the front door with her face set in its usual scowl.

"What is all this racket?" Willadeene said, looking at the screen. "I could hear y'all laughing from my front lawn."

"Why was she in her front yard in the dark?" Lacy whispered to Cami, giggling.

Shelby waved her over. "Movie night, Willadeene, come join us."

Her eyes narrowed as if she didn't entirely trust what was happening, but she shuffled into the living room and plopped down in the armchair next to the window.

"I'm not sitting through this nonsense," Willadeene grumbled. "Christmas movies ain't what they used to be."

Lacy grinned and looked over at her. "Oh, you'll

love the next one. *National Lampoon's Christmas Vacation* is up next."

Willadeene huffed, but Shelby caught the faintest glimmer of amusement in her eyes. She knew Willadeene must have a soft spot for tradition and holiday gatherings, even if she would never say it out loud.

"*It's a Wonderful Life* is the best Christmas movie, and I'll fight anyone who tells me otherwise," Willadeene said, crossing her arms.

Nobody argued with her.

As *Elf* ended, Reed stretched his arms out and returned to the home screen. "Okay, one holiday classic movie down. I guess now we're moving on to *Christmas Vacation.*"

"Finally, a real Christmas movie," Willadeene said, smirking slightly. "Well, at least better than whatever that was. That was just silliness."

"Okay, Willadeene, let's not act like you're too good for *Elf*," Cami teased.

Willadeene waved her off, but Shelby noticed she was settling into the seat more comfortably like she was finally relaxing for the evening.

As *Christmas Vacation* started, the room erupted with laughter. Shelby couldn't help but laugh as Lacy and Cami quoted the lines word for word, laughing at every mishap the main character faced on screen.

"This is me every year," Lacy said, leaning over to Cami as they watched the character try to untangle an impossibly long string of Christmas lights. "Literally every year."

"I've learned not to get involved with lights," Cami said. "You buy one of those pre-lit trees, and you don't have to worry about things like that."

"Speaking of lights, can we all agree that Shelby's tree is the best in town this year?" Lacy said.

"I agree," Reed said. "She even had me rearrange some of the ornaments to make them more symmetrical."

"You're a holiday perfectionist, and I respect it," Cami said, raising her mug in a mock salute.

Even Willadeene cracked a smile at the absurdity of some of the moments in the movie. She tried to hide it by sipping her hot chocolate from her mug. The movie finally finished, and Shelby leaned back against Reed as the room fell into a comfortable silence.

"Well, this is the perfect way to kick off Christmas," Lacy said. "Thank you so much for hosting, Shelby."

"Anytime," she said.

Willadeene stood up from her chair with a groan.

"You know, we could watch just *one* more movie," Shelby said, smiling slyly. It was getting late in the evening, and she was pretty sure nobody would say yes, but to her surprise, everybody sat back down as Reed picked another movie. This was going to be a long but very fun night.

CHAPTER 10

WILLADEENE GRUMBLED under her breath as she shuffled out of the living room. The movie they were watching now was about some kid who got left at home when his parents went out of town at Christmas. Who leaves their kid at home without noticing they're missing? Seemed like a pretty bad case of child neglect if you asked her.

She walked over to the bathroom because her bladder wasn't what it used to be and noticed that somebody was occupying it. She looked back into the living room and saw that Cami was missing. This wasn't fair that somebody was hogging the bathroom, and it seemed like she'd been in there for what felt like an eternity.

Willadeene simply couldn't wait any longer. Her

aging bladder had its own ideas. *These young folks think they can just hog up all the bathrooms*, she muttered to herself. She was sure Shelby wouldn't mind if she snuck upstairs just this once, and she didn't want to interrupt them while they were watching the movie. Then Reed would stop it, and this night would go on even longer. It was hours past her bedtime. Her bladder knew it. The bathroom upstairs would be quieter anyway, and nobody would notice her missing.

She made her way up the stairs, her footsteps soft on the hardwood floor. When she reached the top of the stairs, she noticed the soft glow of a light coming from a slightly ajar door of what she assumed to be the guest room. Her brows furrowed. Shelby hadn't mentioned having any visitors. Maybe she was cleaning it up for somebody coming to stay for the wedding. It would be doing her a favor to turn that light off. Electricity bills were high, after all.

Curiosity got the best of her. She walked toward the bathroom at first, but she just couldn't resist sneaking a peek at the guest room as she passed. She wanted to see how Shelby had decorated it. But what she saw made her freeze in her tracks. Sitting there on the edge of the guest bed, looking at a book, was none other than her sister Gertie. Willadeene felt like her throat was closing. Her mouth dropped open, and for a moment, she couldn't move or speak. Was this what dying felt like? Was she having a heart attack?

Gertie sensed someone watching her and looked up, her face turning pale.

"Willadeene!" she said, putting a hand to her chest.

The sound of her name snapped her out of her trance, and her shock transformed into rage.

"What in God's name are you doing here?" she hissed.

Gertie stood up slowly, raising her hands as if trying to calm her sister down. "Willadeene, please just let me explain."

"Explain what?" she interrupted, her voice rising. "What could you possibly have to say that you haven't said in thirty years? And why are you stalking me? Why are you at Shelby's house? I told you to leave me alone. You should be back in Florida by now, slathering on sunscreen and fighting off alligators."

Gertie's face softened, her eyes pleading. "I told you I just want a chance to talk."

"I told you not to come back here. I told you I didn't want to see you," Willadeene's voice cracked as her anger surged. She was worried about her blood pressure. She was already on pills. It felt as if her head might explode. But what she mainly felt was betrayal. Not only because Gertie was there but also because Shelby had obviously let her stay without telling her.

Before Gertie could say anything else, Willadeene let out a sharp, strangled cry and backed toward the stairs as she wrung her hands.

"You have no right to be here. No right!"

"Willadeene, please listen to me for a second," Gertie begged.

But Willadeene wasn't having it. She turned around, her breath coming more in gasps than normal breaths as she stomped down the stairs.

"Shelby! Shelby!" she yelled.

This caused a commotion downstairs as Shelby, Lacy, Cami, and Reed all jumped up simultaneously, almost knocking over the bowl of popcorn and running toward the foyer.

"Willadeene?" Shelby said when she found her at the bottom of the stairs. "What's going on?"

"I cannot believe you."

Everyone stared at her in confusion.

"What's wrong? What happened?" Shelby said.

"You knew about this." Willadeene's voice was

trembling now as she pointed upstairs. "You knew she was here."

Before Shelby could respond, Gertie stepped to the top of the stairs, her presence now painfully obvious.

"You knew my sister was staying here. You let her do that without telling me?"

Cami and Lacy's mouths dropped open, and Shelby's heart dropped. This was not how this was supposed to go.

"Willadeene, I can explain."

"Explain?" she barked. "You let her stay here? You knew she was here, and you didn't tell me."

"I was going to tell you," Shelby said. "I just thought, well, I thought maybe if you knew she was here, you might consider talking to her. And it's just right before Christmas. There was nowhere else around here for her to stay."

"Talk to her? I already told you I didn't want to talk to her. I don't want anything to do with her."

Cami and Lacy exchanged nervous glances as if they didn't know what to do.

"Willadeene," Gertie said from the top of the stairs. "I just wanted a chance to talk. Please don't take it out on Shelby. She was doing me a favor."

"No," Willadeene said. "I told you to stay away,

and you're not welcome here. You're not welcome in my life. And I'm tired of you butting in."

Shelby felt a wave of guilt wash over her. She had done the wrong thing, obviously.

"I'm sorry," Shelby whispered. "I just thought…"

"Well, you thought wrong," Willadeene snapped, interrupting her. "You had no right to interfere."

Reed walked over slowly, but said nothing at first. Just stood at Shelby's side.

"I want her out of here. I want her out of this house. Out of my life for good."

Gertie was now walking down the stairs, tears spilling over her cheeks.

"Willadeene, I'm begging you. Please don't end things like this."

"Save your tears for someone who cares," Willadeene said coldly. "You're nothing to me anymore. You made sure of that a long time ago."

The silence that followed was thick with tension. Shelby's heart ached for both of them. But there was nothing more that she could do or say. Willadeene was too hurt, too angry. She stormed out the door, grabbing her coat from the hook as Shelby called out after her.

"Please don't leave like this."

But Willadeene didn't respond. She threw the

door open, the cold night air rushing in, and slammed it behind her as she disappeared into the darkness.

"Well," Reed said after a long moment, "that didn't exactly go as planned."

"I'm sorry," Shelby said, looking at Reed and then at Gertie.

"I didn't expect her to forgive me immediately, but I didn't think it would be this bad."

"We'll figure it out," Shelby said. "But not tonight."

For tonight, the damage had been done.

Shelby stood in front of the full-length mirror at the bridal shop. She stared at her reflection with tension in her neck and shoulders. It had only worsened since the previous night's dramatic encounter between Gertie and Willadeene. Her wedding was just days away, and the last thing she needed was even more stress.

"Well?" Shelby said, glancing at the seamstress, Mrs. Fields, a cheerful woman with a rotund figure and silver hair pulled up into a bun. She had a tape measure draped around her neck.

Mrs. Fields stepped back and tilted her head, her brow furrowed. "Um…"

Shelby's heart sank. "Is something wrong?" Lacy asked, sitting on a nearby chaise, flipping through a bridal magazine. She looked up, sensing Shelby's anxiety.

"Well," Mrs. Fields said, walking around Shelby slowly, with her hands gently tugging at the fabric. "It looks like the waistline isn't sitting quite right. Have you gained a little weight since your last fitting, dear?"

Shelby let out a small laugh, though it wasn't out of humor. "Honestly, I've probably put on a few pounds from Christmas desserts. Between the wedding, Willadeene, Gertie, and everything else, I… I've been eating a little more than normal."

Mrs. Fields didn't ask who Gertie or Willadeene were and didn't need to. "No worries. We'll just need to let it out a little bit," Mrs. Fields said, making a quick mark on the dress. "And you're a little bustier than most, so we might have to let this out a little bit, too. When we gain a little weight, our chests seem to grow the fastest," she said, pointing at Shelby's chest. "The hem is fine."

Of course, Shelby thought. She hadn't exactly

gotten taller. Getting taller could've helped the whole big waist and chest situation.

"So, how long will this take?" Shelby asked, trying to keep her voice steady.

Mrs. Fields paused, looking at her in the mirror. "Normally, I'd say a couple of weeks, but given the short notice, I'll try to get it done within the next four or five days."

"Within the next four or five days?" Shelby's heart raced. That felt like an eternity, especially with the wedding so close. "But it will be done by Christmas Eve, right? No problems?"

Mrs. Fields smiled reassuringly. "Oh, dear, it'll be done. I've never let a bride walk down the aisle without her dress being absolutely perfect, and I'm not about to start now."

Lacy stood up and walked over, patting Shelby reassuringly on the shoulder. "You're going to look beautiful, Shelby. This is just a little hiccup."

Shelby forced a smile and nodded, trying to hold back her tears. "I know, it's just… everything feels like it's piling up. First the venue gets destroyed, then Willadeene and Gertie have the whole confrontation, and now my dress needs alterations because I've blown up like a pufferfish. I just wanted the wedding to be perfect, and nothing has gone according to plan. Maybe I can also get PMS and bloat up so bad that I'll have to wear a tarp and waddle down the aisle."

Lacy squeezed her shoulder. "Let me remind you of something. Nothing about life ever goes exactly as we planned, or else I'd still be married to the man I thought was the love of my life. But what really matters is that you are marrying the love of your life. Everything else will fall into place, even if it feels like you have to go through a tornado first."

Shelby took a deep breath and nodded. "I know you're right. It's just hard not to feel overwhelmed."

Mrs. Fields gave Shelby's waist one final tug and stepped back. "There we go. I'll let this out a little, and then you'll be all set. You'll have your dream wedding. You just wait."

Shelby smiled gratefully. She stepped down from the platform and changed back into her regular clothes. The past few weeks had been a whirlwind; all she wanted to do was walk down the aisle and marry Reed without any more surprises. She slipped on her shoes as Lacy sat down beside her.

"You're strong, Shelby. Just hold on a little longer, and everything will work out."

Over the time that she had known Lacy, they had become best friends, and that was not something she had ever dreamed would happen when she met Lacy for the first time at her front door. They didn't seem to have anything in common. They didn't seem to be anything alike, but now she was her rock.

They walked out of the bridal shop, and Shelby glanced up at the sky. The mid-December sun was shining, but she barely felt its warmth.

"Okay, next stop, a stiff drink," Lacy said with a wink.

Shelby laughed, shaking her head. "I wish. I still have a ton of wedding stuff to handle, and I need to go by the bookstore."

"Well, if you change your mind, you know where to find me. I'll be in my kitchen with a bottle of wine and two glasses. Thankfully, my kids are with their grandmother for a few days, so we can drink all the wine you need."

"Thanks, Lacy," Shelby said, giving her a tight hug before getting into her car.

As she drove home, her mind swirled with everything that had gone wrong, but she knew in the end everything would fall into place. It had to. She was marrying Reed. That was the only thing that mattered.

∽

Willadeene stood outside Shelby's house at the front door, her heart pounding in her chest. If all of this stress didn't get out of her system soon, she was going to have to see the cardiologist. She hadn't planned on coming over this morning. In fact, she had planned on doing the exact opposite—staying as far away from her sister as she possibly could. But after the crazy encounter last night during Christmas movie night, she'd barely slept. She felt embarrassed. She felt guilty for yelling at Shelby, who had always been nice to her, even if she was sometimes annoying.

But Gertie's face, her words, and her very presence had invaded Willadeene's mind all night, and she was tired of it. She was going to get this settled once and for all. For three decades, she had built a wall around her heart, a fortress that would keep her sister—or really anyone else—out. The only person she had ever let in was her husband, but he had died years ago now, and nobody else had come past her steel door.

But now Gertie was back, and everything was crumbling, it seemed. She had to fix this. She had to make sure that Gertie didn't worm her way into Shelby's life or the lives of the other women. They were the only real family she had now—Shelby,

Lacy, Joan, and Cami. They were the ones she cared about, even if she never said it. She didn't care about Gertie, or at least that's what she kept telling herself.

She knocked on the door, her knuckles tapping the wood harder than she intended. The door creaked open a few moments later, and there stood Gertie, still wearing her housecoat, looking more fragile in the daylight, her silver hair slightly tousled as if she'd had a restless night, too.

"Willadeene," she said, her voice soft like she wasn't quite sure if she should be scared to see her or happy.

Willadeene's hands tightened into fists at her side. She pushed her way past her into the house. "We need to talk," Willadeene snapped.

Gertie swallowed hard, stepped back, and closed the door. "I know we do. I've been waiting for you to come around."

Willadeene let out a bitter laugh, crossing her arms. "Come around? Oh no, I'm here to tell you to pack up and get out of here. This is my town, not yours."

Gertie's face fell, the glimmer of hope in her eyes completely extinguished. "Willadeene, please, it's early in the morning. Can you settle down?"

"No!" she interrupted. "I'm not interested in

whatever story you've come up with. You've already caused enough damage in my life. You've ruined enough."

"I'm not here to ruin anything," Gertie said, her voice trembling. "I'm here to make things right. I know I hurt you—"

"Make things right?" Willadeene scoffed. "You can't just waltz back into my life after all these years and make things right. You're too late. You were too late when you didn't even bother to show up when I lost my husband. Do you remember that? Do you remember how you were nowhere to be found when I needed you the most?"

Gertie's eyes welled with tears. "I do remember and hate myself for it every day."

"Well, good. You should."

Gertie sucked in a shaky breath and stepped closer. "Willadeene, I didn't stay away because I didn't care. I stayed away because I was ashamed of myself. I was embarrassed. I owed you so much money, and I couldn't face you. I was too much of a coward to show up, and I let my pride keep me away. I know that doesn't excuse it. I was drowning in guilt and didn't know how to fix it."

"You didn't know how to fix it?" Willadeene's voice rose with disbelief. "You could have started by showing up. You could have come to the funeral. That was the very least you could have done. Or picked up the phone or written me a letter—anything."

"I know," Gertie said, tears streaming down her face. "I know, and I'm sorry. I'm genuinely so sorry. I'm here now because I want to make things right. I want to pay you back."

Thirty years ago, Gertie had borrowed a large sum of money from Willadeene and her husband. At the time, they really didn't have it to give, but Willadeene adored her little sister. She couldn't say no, and it had created a rift in her marriage for a short time. Willadeene promised her husband that Gertie would pay it back quickly, but instead, Gertie disappeared. She wouldn't answer calls. She wouldn't answer her door when Willadeene stopped by. After a few months, Willadeene gave up and took a second job to make ends' meet.

"Pay me back?" Willadeene's voice dripped with sarcasm. "What are you talking about?"

"I won the lottery, Willadeene, down in Florida a few months back. The first thing I thought about was how I owed you that money—how I've owed you money for over thirty years. That's why I came back. I want to give it back to you, every single cent plus interest. I'm so embarrassed at how I never paid you back. I don't know why I couldn't come to you back then and apologize or work out a payment schedule. I was just overwhelmed, and I hid from you. It was the worst mistake of my life."

Willadeene blinked, stunned into silence. Her mind raced. She had been expecting excuses or lies, but this was different. "Wait," she said, narrowing her eyes. "You won the lottery?"

Gertie nodded as she held back a slight smile. "Yes, and I want to use it to fix things. I won over two million dollars. I know money can't change what happened, but it's a start. I'll pay you back what I owe you and then some. I want to make sure you're taken care of."

Willadeene's mouth tightened. "I don't want your money."

Gertie's eyes widened. "Please, Willadeene, let me do this. Let me help you. Some of that is your money."

"I don't need your help," she said, her voice rising. "I needed your help years ago when I lost the love of my life. I've never been the same. I needed your help when I was drowning in his medical bills. When I was barely scraping by, but you weren't there. You didn't care then, and I don't want you to swoop in now with your lottery winnings like you're saving me."

"I know I failed you. I know I let you down, but I'm here now, and I'm trying. We used to be so close. Please let me do this one thing. Let me try to fix what I've broken."

Willadeene stared at her sister, the years of bitterness and resentment swirling inside her like a storm. She'd spent so many years hating Gertie and blaming her for abandoning her when she needed her, blaming her for borrowing money and never paying it back, blaming her for making Willadeene's financial life so much harder when she needed that money. But now, hearing the pain in Gertie's voice and seeing the desperation in her eyes, Willadeene suddenly felt something shift inside her.

She didn't want Gertie's money. She didn't want an apology. What she wanted—and what she had always wanted—was her sister back. But she didn't know if that was possible.

"I don't know if I can do this," Willadeene whispered, her voice barely audible.

Gertie reached out, her hand trembling as she put it on Willadeene's arm. It was the first time her sister had touched her in decades. "Look, you don't have to forgive me right now. I just want the chance to be your sister again. I've missed you so much, Willadeene. Please let me try."

Willadeene's throat suddenly tightened, her vision blurring with tears that she had never allowed herself to shed over the years. She wanted to push Gertie away and cling to the anger that had protected her for so long. It was comfortable, even if it was painful. But something inside of her was breaking. The wall was starting to crumble, and she couldn't rebuild it fast enough.

"I don't know," she said again, her voice cracking.

Gertie nodded, tears streaming down her face. "That's okay. I'm not going anywhere. I will wait as long as it takes."

Willadeene stood there, her heart torn between the pain of the past and a tiny bit of fragile hope for the future. She didn't know if she could ever forgive Gertie, but for the first time in a long time, she thought she might be willing to try.

CHAPTER 11

Lacy's beautifully designed kitchen was filled with the smell of freshly baked gingerbread and the sound of laughter as the four women gathered around her large kitchen island. It was festive and lively with Christmas music playing in the background and the lights from her Christmas tree visible from the living room.

"So, what's the prize again for this gingerbread competition?" Cami asked, raising an eyebrow. She was leaning over her pre-built structure with an icing bag in her hand.

Lacy smiled, "Bragging rights, and maybe a gift card to my favorite coffee shop—but mostly bragging rights."

"Oh, I'm all in for bragging rights," Shelby said,

adjusting her apron as she looked at the pile of candy laid out before her. She always liked coming to Lacy's house. It was so beautiful and well-appointed, unlike her own house, which was kind of eclectic. "Now, don't underestimate my gingerbread skills. Reed thinks I'm a pro."

Joan laughed as she carefully put icing on the roof of her house. "Well, I'm just trying to keep mine from collapsing. It's been a while since I've done anything this intricate. My hands are shaking."

Lacy shook her head. "No excuses, Joan. You've got this."

The women settled into their tasks, each of them focusing on building their best gingerbread house. Cami added intricate icing details to the windows, while Shelby stuck candy canes along the edges of hers, giving them a whimsical holiday feel.

As they worked, the conversation naturally shifted toward the topic of Willadeene and Gertie.

"So, how are things going with Willadeene and her sister?" Cami asked, still focusing on her master-piece. "I haven't heard much since the movie night explosion."

Shelby sighed, squeezing out a swirl of icing onto the roof. "They've had a few conversations since then. Willadeene still doesn't seem to be sure what she wants to do, though. I think she's torn between staying angry—which is much more comfortable for her—or letting Gertie back into her life. Vulnerability isn't exactly Willadeene's strong suit."

"I can't imagine what it must be like after all that time," Joan said, trying to rebuild a section of her house. "Trying to rebuild a sister relationship after so much hurt."

"Exactly," Shelby said. "But they're spending time together, and Willadeene won't admit it, but I think part of her is enjoying it. I think part of her wants to reconcile, but it's just so hard for her to admit when she's wrong."

Lacy put her icing bag on the counter. "You know, sometimes it's easier for us to stay angry. It feels safer."

"That's true," Cami said.

"You have to believe in second chances, especially around the holidays. Although, there were no second chances with my marriage," Lacy added, laughing.

"Yeah, it's that Christmas miracle kind of thinking," Cami said, smiling. "But seriously, maybe they just need a little more time."

"I sure hope so," Shelby said. "I've done everything I can. I want to see Willadeene happy."

"What would that be like?" Lacy asked, laughing. "I feel like it'd be the eighth wonder of the world."

The conversation shifted again, moving on to wedding details and Christmas plans as the gingerbread houses started to take their final forms. Each one was uniquely decorated, reflecting the personality of its builder. When they finished, Lacy snapped a photo of each house on her phone and posted them on social media. She didn't identify who made which one but asked people to vote for the next couple of hours.

"You know I'm going to win," Cami said confidently.

"Well, we'll see," Lacy said, raising her eyebrow.

"I think they're all winners," Joan said.

"You're always so nice, Joan," Shelby said, patting her shoulder. "Okay, ladies, may the best gingerbread architect win. Let's go drink wine while we wait."

The night was filled with laughter as the votes started coming in. Each of them kept checking their phones, looking at the increasing tally. Shelby took a sip of hot cocoa after realizing she had already had too many glasses of wine. She leaned against the counter, watching her friends with a smile. These were the moments she cherished—no wedding stress, no drama, just pure fun and Christmas cheer.

As the night wore on, the notifications began to pick up. "Look at this!" Lacy said, holding up her phone. "People are calling my house a 'gingerbread castle.' I love it."

Joan chuckled softly. "I'm just hoping mine doesn't collapse before the voting is over."

A new notification popped up, and Lacy squealed. "Looks like we have a winner, ladies. I hate to say it, but my masterpiece officially won the poll."

Cami threw her hands in the air dramatically. "It's rigged! I demand a recount," she said, laughing.

"Well, Lacy, it's your moment. Enjoy your bragging rights. You earned them, and I guess we owe you a gift card to your coffee shop."

Lacy grabbed a wooden spoon from the counter and raised it in the air like a trophy. "I'd like to thank all of my supporters, my fans, and the steady hand that God gave me to place those gumdrops with precision. You all doubted me, but I persevered!" she said, bowing her head dramatically.

The group dissolved into laughter as Lacy strutted around the kitchen in her Christmas pajamas, still holding her "trophy." Even though it was all in fun, Shelby could tell how much the evening meant to all of them. It was one of the last chances they'd get to be together like this before Joan moved away.

No matter what their personal struggles, they were the best of friends. And that was something Shelby had never expected to happen so late in her life. She'd never had a tight circle of friends like this, but now she couldn't imagine life without them.

As the night wound down with hot cocoa, they sat together in the living room, the lights from the Christmas tree casting a warm glow over everything. Joan looked out the window and sighed contentedly. "This is what we all needed—a little Christmas magic."

Cami nodded. "Yeah, it's been a wild few months, but this is why I love this time of year. It's just the feeling that you get."

"Here's to more moments like this," Shelby said, raising her cup of cocoa. "And maybe next year, we can crown someone else 'Gingerbread Queen.'"

"Good luck with that," Lacy smirked. "Because I've already got ideas for next year."

As the night came to a close, they hugged each other and said their goodbyes. Shelby, with her gingerbread house box in hand, smiled as she walked out onto the sidewalk and turned toward home.

Graystone was festive and bustling, the kind of Christmas joy that could light up the darkest of days. Reed had a beautiful restaurant, and Shelby loved going there. The scent of fresh rolls, baked ham, and warm cinnamon filled the air. Children were all over the place laughing. The smallest were toddlers, and the oldest were teenagers.

The soft murmur of holiday music played in the background, and occasionally, Shelby heard a bell ringing from the kitchen so someone could pick up an order. Reed had really outdone himself this year, hosting the annual toy event for foster children. It was a tradition that was quickly becoming one of Shelby's favorite parts of the holiday season.

Shelby, Lacy, and Cami stood near the entrance, watching as social workers brought in groups of foster children. The younger ones' eyes were wide with excitement as they looked around, especially when they saw Santa Claus sitting in a large ornate chair in the corner. Christmas lights hung everywhere, and garlands framed the windows. The centerpiece of the room was a large Christmas tree that was fully decked out in ornaments and tinsel, and under the tree was a huge pile of gifts, each one carefully wrapped and labeled for the children attending today's event.

"Look at their little faces," Lacy said, her eyes soft as she smiled at a little boy who stood in front of the Christmas tree with his mouth hanging open. "This is what Christmas is all about."

"Reed really went all out," Shelby said, her heart swelling with pride. He had insisted on closing the restaurant for the afternoon to host the event, turning it into a magical wonderland just for these kids. "I'm so glad he wanted to do this here."

"Me too," Cami said, glancing over at the buffet table lined with plates of food. "He even made sure to have kid-friendly food. I mean, look at those chicken fingers and the mac and cheese. He's a genius."

They all laughed, but Shelby couldn't help but feel a deep sense of gratitude for the man she was about to marry. It wasn't just that he made her happy, but planning this perfect event and seeing how much he cared for their community, especially the children, made her love him even more. She couldn't wait to be the mother of his children.

Santa greeted children as they arrived, asking them about their Christmas wishes. The sight of Santa Claus always brought a little flutter of joy to

Shelby's heart, and she had never lost it as she got older.

"I think I'm gonna go help over there with the gift table," Lacy said, walking toward a table near the tree where social workers were organizing the presents by name. "I can start handing the gifts out once Santa is ready. I've always wanted to be an elf," she laughed.

"I'll help with the food," Cami said. "Keep an eye on the buffet, make sure it stays stocked." Reed was also allowing some of the adults to order things from the kitchen, which is why that bell kept ringing in the back. He figured they probably didn't want to eat chicken fingers and mac and cheese.

Shelby was feeling a little bit hungry, so she decided to order a sandwich in a little while. "How's it going, chef?" she said as she approached him.

He grinned. "It's going great. Look at all these kids. They're having the time of their lives."

"They really are," she said, looking around the room. "You did an amazing job with this."

"It was a team effort," he said, shrugging. "Besides, you know I'm a sucker for Christmas. This is the highlight of my year."

She leaned up on her tiptoes and kissed him on the cheek. "You've made this Christmas even more special for me and all these kids. They're never going to forget this."

They stood side by side for a moment, watching the children as they lined up for Santa, their little faces glowing with excitement.

"I love doing this. These kids don't get enough good memories, and if we can give them even one great Christmas, then it's all worth it. But I have to admit something."

"What?" she asked.

"I can't wait to play Santa Claus for our kids."

She smiled. "I can't wait for that either."

The afternoon continued as the event unfolded perfectly. Lacy had set up the gift station by the tree and helped hand out presents with Santa Claus. Wide-eyed children walked by to receive their presents and then immediately ran to the other side of the room to open them. Cami floated around the room, making sure each child had whatever they needed to eat or drink. She even made special hot cocoa with lots of extra marshmallows.

"Next up is Sarah," Santa boomed, holding up a brightly wrapped package. A young girl who looked to be no more than seven years old bounced up to him, her eyes wide as she accepted the gift from his hands.

"This one is for me?" she asked, her voice small and filled with wonder.

"Just for you, Sarah," Santa said warmly.

Her eyes lit up as she tore into the wrapping paper, revealing a brand-new doll. She squealed with delight and hugged the doll to her chest before running back to sit on the floor and play with it.

"Okay, I'm getting emotional," Lacy said as she wiped a tear from the corner of her eye. "This is too much. It's so hard to think that these kids don't have their own families to celebrate Christmas with. I hope each and every one of them gets adopted as soon as possible. And I hope their foster parents are amazing in the meantime."

"I do, too," Shelby said, her heart clenching. If it was up to her, she would adopt every single one of them right now. Although she didn't think her house was quite big enough for that. It made her sad to think that there were so many children in the world who had come from bad situations and ended up in foster care. Sure, some of them probably had wonderful foster parents, but there were a lot of them who didn't. There were a lot of them who would age out of the system and never have a family at all.

She tried not to think about it because it was such a joyful day.

Cami joined them by the tree. "I wish we could do this every day, but I also wish there weren't this many kids in foster care around here."

The afternoon passed in a blur of joy and laughter, sadness and hope. Every child who received a gift seemed to light up the room even more, and pretty soon, the restaurant was just filled with the sound of them playing with their new toys and laughing.

Once the day was over, Shelby felt such a deep sense of fulfillment.

"Thanks again, Reed," one of the social workers said as she shook his hand. "You made this such a special day for these kids. I hope we can work together again."

"Anytime," Reed said. "We don't have to wait until Christmas. Why don't we plan something for this summer? Maybe Christmas in July?"

She smiled broadly. "Really? That would be wonderful. I'll be in touch."

After the last of the kids had left, Lacy, Cami, and Shelby helped Reed clean up the restaurant. It didn't take long, but by the time everything was put in its place, they were all exhausted.

"Well, that was a perfect day," Cami said, wiping down one of the tables. "I don't think I've ever seen so many smiles in one place."

"I'm going to be riding this high for the rest of the week," Lacy said, smiling. "But for now, I want to go home and hug my kids."

Shelby leaned against one of the booths, her arms crossed. "Thank you for doing this, Reed. You've really made today so special."

He kissed her on top of the head. "You helped too, and you know this is just the beginning. We're going to have so many more Christmases like this, Shelby. Full of love, family, and all the good things."

"And I can't wait," she said, smiling.

Willadeene stood at her kitchen counter with her hands gripping the edges of the countertop like she was going to break the granite between her fingers. The coffee was brewing in her old machine, which she'd had for years. She was a creature of habit and didn't like many things to change. Sometimes, the older things worked better anyway.

The familiar gurgling sound filled the silence in her kitchen, but there was no comfort in that sound like there usually was. Instead, her stomach was twisted into knots. She felt like she had a million butterflies flying around in there. She hadn't felt this nervous in years, but then again, she also hadn't invited her estranged sister over for coffee in three decades.

She looked around the room at the small table by the window where two mismatched mugs sat waiting. The tension in her shoulders only seemed to grow as she thought about the conversation they would have. She had no idea how this would go, whether they would end up in yet another argument, or if they could even sit in the same room without it turning ugly. Of course, she was well aware that she was the one who usually turned it ugly. Gertie had been on her best behavior, but then again, that was Gertie. Her younger sister had always been quieter, shy, and introverted. Willadeene had never been any of those things.

The doorbell rang, cutting through her thoughts. She inhaled sharply and straightened herself before making her way to the front door. She stopped for a second with her hand on the doorknob, trying to calm her nerves. Then she slowly exhaled and pulled the door open. Gertie stood there, looking smaller than Willadeene remembered the day before. Her hair had turned so silver over the years. In Willadeene's mind, she was still her little sister. In her mind's eye, she could see her running around out in their yard as a kid, chasing butterflies or kicking a ball. She had the darkest brown hair back in those days, but now it was snow white, and the lines on her face were much deeper, more pronounced. Of course, when Willadeene looked in the mirror, she saw much the same thing. Although she had held on to dyeing her hair for many years, it was only about five years ago that she'd stopped, and now her hair was as white as snow, too.

"Come in," Willadeene said, stepping aside and letting Gertie into the house. Her tone was still curt, but she was working on it. Warm and welcoming wasn't exactly what anyone would describe her as, anyway. Gertie gave a tentative smile and then stepped into the small foyer.

"Thank you."

They walked into the kitchen, where the smell of coffee filled the air. Willadeene pointed at Gertie to sit at the table and then poured them two cups of coffee. She set a carton of creamer in the middle of them, and of course, her favorite sugar bowl already sat there. It belonged to their mother, crystal and beautiful, just like her mother.

"Is this Mama's sugar bowl?" Gertie asked, touching it and staring.

"Yes, it is. One of the few things I got. Mama wasn't known for keeping a lot of things."

Gertie smiled. "No, she wasn't. If I remember correctly, there's a little chip in the glass right here," she said, touching the very tip of the handle.

"Yes, it's still there. I remember when she did that. Dropped a dinner plate on top of it at Thanksgiving. She was so mad. She loved this sugar bowl."

"Where's the creamer pitcher?"

Willadeene shrugged her shoulders. "I never found it. Maybe she broke it somewhere along the way and just didn't tell us."

"Well, she was getting a lot of dementia by the time she passed away," Gertie said. "There's no telling what happened to it."

They sat there in silence for a few moments, not making eye contact as they each sipped their coffee. Willadeene had to admit that even that little bit of conversation about times gone by settled her nerves a bit. There was an awkwardness that shouldn't have been there between sisters, but it was what it was.

"I wasn't sure if you'd actually invite me over," Gertie said.

"Well, I wasn't sure I would either," Willadeene said.

"I'm glad you did."

Gertie looked around the room. "I love your kitchen. Your curtains are adorable with the little strawberries on them."

"I sewed those myself many years ago."

"Really? That's very impressive. I didn't know you sewed."

"Well, you wouldn't know a lot of things about me after missing the last three decades, would you?"

Willadeene felt bad about saying it as soon as it came out of her mouth. She was supposed to be trying, but sometimes her mouth just got away from her.

"Sorry."

"It's okay. I understand."

"I don't know if this is going to work, Gertie. I really don't."

"Well, there's no rush."

Willadeene chuckled under her breath. "I would say there's a bit of a rush. Neither one of us is getting any younger."

Gertie smiled. The silence stretched on, and then Gertie's gaze wandered to a bookshelf in the corner, her eyes landing on a worn, leather-bound album.

"Is that our old family album?"

Willadeene followed her gaze. It hadn't been touched in years, but she could tell her about every photo inside of it like the back of her hand.

"I haven't looked at that in a very long time," Willadeene said.

"May I?"

She hesitated with her fingers tightening around her coffee mug before nodding. Gertie stood up and walked over, picking up the album from the shelf and then sitting back at the table. She flipped it open to the first page, and Willadeene's breath caught in her throat. The images greeted her like a warm hug and a slap in the face at the same time. Their parents, young and full of life, smiling in the garden of their childhood home. And the two sisters themselves, grinning in the front yard, arms slung across each other's shoulders like nothing would ever come between them.

Willadeene watched Gertie as she traced a finger over one of the photos. "Do you remember this? Mama had just made us those matching dresses, and we hated them."

Willadeene smiled slightly. "I hated the lace. It was so itchy."

"We made such a fuss about those dresses, but we

wore them anyway because we didn't want to hurt her feelings. Plus, she probably would have pulled a switch off the bush and smacked us right across the legs if we'd said anything out loud."

Willadeene nodded, her chest tightening at the memory. They turned the page, and there was a picture of their father, so big and broad, standing proudly beside the swing he had built for the two of them in the backyard. Willadeene felt a lump form in her throat. She remembered how he used to push her in that swing for hours, and she would laugh and laugh until her throat hurt.

"He was so proud of that swing," Gertie said. "He spent days building it."

Willadeene nodded. "Yes. It took him a long time to build that thing. He kept running into problems. I remember one day, I heard him out there cussing at it. I'd never heard Daddy say a bad word in my life."

They continued flipping through the pages, each picture stirring up memories, some good and some bittersweet. There was a photo of their mother baking in the kitchen, with flour dust on her apron, and there was another picture of the two of them at Christmas time, smiling with excitement as they unwrapped presents.

For a moment, it felt like they were just two

regular sisters again, reminiscing about the life they had shared together. Willadeene found her heart softening, and the walls that she had built around it started to crumble. Then she remembered that their relationship had fallen apart for thirty years. She closed the album with a sharp snap, startling Gertie.

"You know, this doesn't change anything. Just because we shared good times doesn't mean I can forget what you did. You left me when I needed you. I was alone after my husband died, and you didn't even care."

Gertie's face fell. "I've told you so many times that I'm sorry. I don't know what else to say. I'm ashamed. I didn't find out for weeks after your husband died, and I didn't know how to face you after everything. I let too much time pass, and then it just felt like it was insurmountable. But I never stopped thinking about you, Willadeene. I never stopped missing you. For goodness sake, I have your picture sitting on my nightstand."

Willadeene's jaw tightened so much that it felt like it might break under the pressure. "Missing me doesn't make up for all the years you were gone."

"I know it doesn't," Gertie whispered, "but I'm here now, and I'm trying to make things right."

She wanted to believe her. She wanted to let go

of the anger that had weighed her down for so long. "I don't know if I can trust you. I don't know if you'll be gone the next time I need you."

Gertie reached across the table and placed her hand over Willadeene's. "You don't have to trust me right away, but just give me a chance. Let me show you that I'm here for you. I'm not going anywhere."

She looked down at their hands. Part of her wanted to pull away to keep her walls up, but another part, the part that remembered the love they had shared, wanted to try. Maybe it was something about seeing pictures of her parents, but she knew without a shadow of a doubt that they would want her to try. They would want their girls to be together for the rest of their lives.

She let out a shaky breath. "I'm not a very trusting person, Gertie."

She nodded. "That's okay. We'll take it one step at a time. I'm not asking for everything to be fixed overnight. I just want us to try."

Willadeene sat there for a moment. "All right," she said quietly, "one step at a time."

CHAPTER 12

THE AIR in downtown Charleston was crisp but not freezing as Shelby strolled hand-in-hand with Reed. They were walking through the bustling streets lit up with the glow of Christmas lights strung in every direction from all the lampposts. The annual Christmas parade was in full swing, and there was palpable excitement in the air.

Families lined the streets as children bounced with anticipation. Float after float passed by, and the smell of roasted chestnuts and cinnamon flew through the air from the nearby booths, which were lined up on the sidewalks selling everything from Christmas ornaments to hand-knitted sweaters.

Shelby looked at Reed, who was smiling at her, and squeezed his hand. Her heart was so overwhelmed with happiness right now, not just from the holiday season but from their wedding, which was coming up just days from now. She couldn't believe how quickly it was approaching. Lacy had spent all of her time recently trying to ensure everything was perfect. Shelby offered to help, but Lacy and Reed wouldn't hear of it. She had never expected him to get so involved, but he had.

She felt a sudden warm rush of happiness as the parade continued passing by. She thought about how she and Reed would be standing here with their little family all bundled up in future years. It didn't get particularly cold in Charleston, even during the holidays, compared to many places anyway. But thoughts of standing on the sidewalk with her little ones bundled up in their Christmas sweaters made her smile.

She was mixed with excitement and nervousness about her wedding, of course. Nothing ever went completely as planned. Given the fact that she'd already seen her wedding venue get damaged and her dress not fit, she was worried about what else might be coming, but she had decided not to let it upset her. This was going to be the most special day of her life, no matter what, and she was determined to enjoy it. Even though it wasn't the wedding she had initially planned, it would be perfect in its own unique way.

"It's so beautiful tonight, isn't it?" Reed said, looking up at the lights draped down the street.

"Yes, it is," she said. "I love Christmas in Charleston. It's so festive without being too cold."

She looked over her shoulder, scanning the crowd until her eyes landed on Willadeene and Gertie. The sisters were standing a little ways back from the crowd, and Shelby couldn't believe they were together. She felt a little knot of anxiety but some hope as she watched them. They had been spending more time together over the last week, but every interaction still seemed a little cautious, as if they were both waiting for the other shoe to drop.

Of course, Willadeene had her arms crossed tightly over her chest as she surveyed the parade. Her face was always pinched together, and Shelby knew now why she had some of the wrinkles that she had. Gertie stood beside her, looking more at ease but glancing over at her sister occasionally as if checking to see if she was still welcome there. There was still so much hurt between them. That much was obvious.

"Do you think they're going to be okay?" Shelby asked, nodding over toward Willadeene and Gertie.

Reed looked in the same direction, his brow furrowing. "I hope so. It's hard to say, but I know you're doing everything possible to help them."

Shelby sighed. "I just want them to find some peace. It's so hard to watch them be distant when I know how close they used to be."

"They'll figure it out," Reed said. "You've done more than enough to give them a chance at reconciliation."

She smiled at him, grateful for his calm demeanor. He always had a way of putting her at ease, even when she felt completely overwhelmed.

They walked closer to the parade route and spotted Lacy, Cami, and Joan standing at the booth selling hot cocoa and gingerbread cookies. Lacy waved them over, a big smile on her face.

"Hey, we saved you guys a spot," she said.

"Thanks," Shelby said, taking a steaming cup of hot cocoa from Lacy. Even Joan, who had been packing up her house, seemed relaxed and happy tonight.

"I can't believe how adorable this is," Cami said. "It's like something out of a Hallmark movie."

"That's Charleston for you," Joan said, laughing. "They always go all out for the holidays. I sure am going to miss this."

Christmas carols played from the speakers set up along the parade route, and children ran around with glow sticks and light-up necklaces. Floats passed by slowly, each one more colorful and holiday-filled than the last. There were dancing elves, gingerbread houses, and even a giant reindeer with blinking lights on its antlers.

A group of children on one of the floats passed by as they stood there, tossing candy into the crowd. Shelby bent down and picked up a stray candy cane that had landed at her feet, handing it to a little girl who was standing nearby.

"Here you go," she said with a smile.

"Thank you!" the little girl chirped, her face lighting up as she ran back to her parents.

Shelby cherished these simple joys, finding them to be the highlights of the holiday season. It was the sense of community and those little moments that made everything feel so magical, filling her heart with warmth and happiness.

"So how are you feeling about the wedding? Just a few days away now," Lacy asked.

Shelby laughed. "Honestly, I'm feeling a little bit of everything. Overwhelmed, excited, nervous, you name it."

"You're going to make a beautiful bride, and I know it will be perfect."

"I sure hope so," Shelby said, glancing over at Reed, who was deep in conversation with Joan. "I just want everything to go smoothly."

"It will," Cami said, chiming in, handing her a cookie covered in sprinkles. "And if anything goes wrong, just remember, at the end of the day, you're still going to be married to the love of your life."

Shelby took a bite of the cookie and smiled. "You're right. That's all that really matters."

Willadeene stood at the base of the ladder to the attic, staring up at the open hatch. It had been many years since she had even thought about putting her feet on that little ladder and climbing up, but the Christmas decorations were up there, and now she and Gertie needed to get them down. She wasn't sure if she could go through with it, though.

"I can get them down if you don't feel like climbing," Gertie said. "I mean, I *am* the younger sister."

Willadeene pursed her lips, glancing over at her. She wasn't sure if it was harder to think about doing Christmas without her husband yet again or doing something as close as decorating with Gertie after so many years of hurt between them. But Gertie was standing in the hallway with her, offering to help in any way.

"I don't mind," Gertie said, stepping toward the ladder.

Willadeene gave a slight nod, and Gertie began climbing. She watched as she pulled down the old dusty boxes, handing them down one by one. As each box landed at her feet, Willadeene felt the weight of the memories pressing against her heart. Christmas had always been her husband's favorite holiday, and decorating had been a tradition they shared. Once he died, the joy for that season had been buried with him, and she had not decorated since.

"I don't know if I can do this," Willadeene whispered under her breath as Gertie climbed back down, putting the last box at her feet.

Gertie put a hand on her shoulder. "We don't have to do it all today. We'll take our time."

Willadeene swallowed hard and nodded. "It's just... it's been so long. He loved Christmas, you know. It's hard to think about putting up this tree again without him. It's been so many years."

"I know," Gertie said. "I remember how much he

loved it. You two were like kids when it came to Christmas."

Willadeene's lips twitched into a small, sad smile. "He used to string lights everywhere. I used to yell at him and tell him he was going to burn the house down with all those plugs, and he'd laugh and say, 'The more lights, the better. That way, Jesus can find us easier!'"

Gertie chuckled. "Oh, I can picture it. He was always trying to make everything brighter."

They stood there for a moment in the quiet.

"I really miss him," Willadeene said. It was the first time she'd said that out loud in many years, even to herself. Her eyes filled with tears against her will.

"I know you do," Gertie said, reaching over and taking both of her hands. To Willadeene's surprise, she didn't pull away. "But remember that you loved Christmas when we were kids, too. You loved putting up the tree with Mama and Daddy, so maybe you can remember some of those things while we're doing this and not focus so much on your grief."

"I miss all of them," Willadeene said. "Getting old is for the birds."

"But we're very blessed that we get to do it. Some

people aren't so lucky," Gertie said. "Now, come on, let's go get this done."

Together, they carried the boxes into the living room. The room felt bigger than usual, emptier, and Willadeene couldn't help but feel a sense of dread creeping up her spine. She hadn't even seen this tree in this room since her husband passed, and now she was about to pull it out of the box. Much like Shelby, she was allergic to a real Christmas tree, and the one in this box was many decades old. She wasn't sure that it would even stand up anymore.

They opened the boxes, carefully pulling out the old artificial tree. Piece by piece, they started assembling it. Willadeene's hands shook a bit as she fluffed out the branches. All of the memories of past Christmases seemed to flood her mind.

Once they reached for the ornaments, Gertie paused, looking at one of the boxes. "Is that another old family album?"

"Yeah, we loved looking through it at Christmas. He would always joke at how young we all looked."

"Do you mind if I look at it?" Gertie asked, her voice hesitant.

Willadeene hadn't opened that album in years. The thought of looking through it without her husband beside her felt like ripping open an old wound, but something in Gertie's eyes made her nod yes.

Gertie pulled the album out of the box, and they both sat down on the couch with the half-decorated tree standing in the corner. As they flipped through the pages, looking at pictures of themselves as kids with their parents and then eventually with Willadeene and her husband together, the memories were overwhelming.

"He always looked so happy," Gertie said softly. "You two had something special. I never found that myself."

"We did have something special," Willadeene said, her eyes lingering on the picture.

They turned to another page and saw a picture of themselves from years ago with their arms slung around each other's shoulders in front of that very same Christmas tree they were now decorating.

"Oh my gosh, do you remember this?" Gertie asked, smiling. "We couldn't stop laughing because the Christmas tree stand broke, and the tree kept falling over. See how it's leaning?"

Willadeene chuckled, a genuine laugh bubbling up out of her despite herself. "Oh yeah, I remember that. You insisted on trying to fix that stupid stand, and you tried to do it with scotch tape."

Gertie laughed. "Those were good times."

Willadeene nodded, her heart aching. There had been good times before everything went wrong, before hurt and betrayal and grief and loss. She looked over at her sister, seeing the same woman she'd grown up with but also someone who had changed. Maybe they both had.

"I want to ask you something," Gertie said after they closed the album. Her expression looked serious.

Willadeene raised an eyebrow. "What?"

Gertie took in a deep breath. "I've been thinking about this a lot, and I know we've got a lot of history between us, but I was wondering if you'd consider something."

"Consider what?"

"Well... letting me stay here. I mean, permanently."

Willadeene blinked, taken aback. "Stay here? You mean to live here with me?"

Gertie nodded. "We're getting older, Willadeene. Neither one of us has kids, and I don't want to be alone anymore. I know I haven't been there for you like I should have been, but I want to make up for that. We could help each other."

Willadeene's heart started to race. She didn't

know what this mixture of emotions was that she was feeling, but it was very unsettling. She hadn't lived with anyone since her husband had passed, and the idea of sharing her home with Gertie, of all people, was both terrifying and strangely comforting.

"I don't know. That's a big change."

"I know," Gertie said gently, "but we're family, and we've lost so much time making memories. I don't want to waste any more of it. We could care for each other, just like we did when we were kids."

Willadeene stared at her sister. Could she trust Gertie again? Could they really live together after everything that had happened?

Gertie reached into her purse and pulled out a check. "And this. I know we've talked about it already, but I want you to have this. It's the money I owe you plus interest. It's not just about the money. I want you to know I'm serious about making things right."

Willadeene looked down at the check in her sister's hand and then back at Gertie's face. Her eyes were so sincere. It was undeniable. She realized at this moment that maybe it was time to finally let go of her anger.

"I'll think about it," Willadeene said finally.

Gertie smiled. "That's all I ask."

They sat there in silence for a while longer, both of them tired and wondering if they should continue decorating the tree or maybe take a little nap. That was what age could do to you, but it was also a type of freedom that Willadeene enjoyed. If she needed a nap, she was going to take one, and later, with her sister, she could finish decorating the tree.

Shelby sat across her kitchen table from Reed, trying her best to keep her excitement under wraps. They had just finished dinner, some wonderful steaks on the grill and baked potatoes. While Reed sat relaxing, enjoying the last of his glass of wine, Shelby could barely keep sit still. The secret she'd kept for the past few weeks was about to burn a hole through her.

She looked over at the butler's pantry, where Leanne, Reed's sister, had been hiding for the last hour. The timing had to be perfect. He thought that she wouldn't be able to attend the wedding and that she was in Switzerland for business, and she had been. But they had worked it out for her to come home for the week of their wedding.

Reed looked up from his glass and raised an eyebrow. "What's going on with you? You've seemed fidgety all night," he said. "You're not getting cold feet about marrying me, are you?"

She tried to play it off, smoothing the napkin in her lap. "I'm not fidgety," she said, her voice too high-pitched to sound natural. She cleared her throat and took a sip of water. "And maybe it's just that I have a special wedding surprise for you."

"Oh, a surprise?" Reed leaned back in his chair, now fully intrigued. "What have you done, Shelby Anderson?"

She smiled, unable to hold it back any longer. "Okay, don't move. Stay right here." She pushed back from the table and stood up.

He gave her a curious look but followed instructions and stayed in his chair, his eyes following her as she hurried across the kitchen. Taking a deep breath, she pushed open the door and motioned for Leanne to follow her.

"Ready?"

Leanne nodded. "Let's do it."

Shelby stepped back into the dining room, her heart racing as she looked at Reed. "Okay, so I know you thought Leanne wasn't going to be able to make it to the wedding, but..." She motioned towards the pantry and out stepped Leanne, smiling.

Reed's eyes widened in disbelief as he quickly stood up from the chair. "Leanne," he said, his voice filled with shock. She crossed the room laughing as Reed pulled her into a tight hug. "I thought you were stuck in Switzerland. It's not a bad place to be stuck, but I didn't think you'd make it here for the wedding."

"I wanted it to be a surprise," she said, pulling back and grinning at him. "Shelby's been helping me plan this for a few weeks."

He turned to Shelby. "So you did this?"

She shrugged, a pleased smile on her face. "I know how much you wanted her to be here. I couldn't let you get married without your sister by your side."

He turned and wrapped his arms around her, kissing her forehead. "My future wife is amazing," he whispered. "I don't know how you pulled it off, but thank you."

Leanne laughed and leaned against the kitchen counter, watching them. "It wasn't easy keeping the secret, let me tell you. You even called me a couple of weeks ago, laying that big guilt trip on me."

"Yeah, sorry about that," Reed said, chuckling.

Shelby smiled, resting her head against his chest for a moment. "Well, now that you have your big surprise, I think I can finally relax."

He laughed and kissed the top of her head before pulling away. "Oh no, you don't get to relax just yet." He pulled his phone from his pocket and texted someone.

She looked at him, confused. "Excuse me, what are you talking about?"

His eyes looked mischievous as he walked toward the front door. "You're not the only one with surprises, Shelby," he said, looking out the window before turning the doorknob.

Her heart skipped a beat as the door swung open. Her mother, Mona, stood on the porch, looking healthy and well.

Shelby's mouth dropped open in shock, her eyes immediately filling with tears. "Mama," she whispered, barely able to process what she saw.

Mona stepped inside, her face lit up with a smile. "Hey, sweetheart," she said, her voice soft.

Shelby didn't hesitate; she ran across the room and threw her arms around her mother, holding her tightly. "I can't believe you're here. You're supposed to be in Tennessee. I thought you were too sick to travel. Are you sure you're okay?"

Mona pulled back just enough to look at her. "I'm on a new medication. It's been working wonders, and when Reed reached out, I wasn't going to miss your wedding. He offered to make plans and pay for me to get here, so here I am. I've been waiting in the car until just the right moment."

Shelby looked between Reed and her mother. "So you did this?" she said.

He nodded and smiled. "I knew how much it would mean to have your mom here. She said she felt good enough to travel, and I trusted her, so I figured this was a great way to surprise you."

She wiped away her tears, laughing. "I just don't know what to say."

"You don't have to say anything. Just enjoy the moment."

Leanne clapped her hands together from the other side of the room. "Surprises are so much fun! Now, where do you keep your wine?"

Shelby turned to her mother. She looked stronger than she had in a very long time. "You look amazing, Mama. I can't believe you're really here."

Mona chuckled. "I'm here, baby, and I'm so proud of you. I wouldn't have missed this for the world, even if I had to watch it on video chat. I was going to be here. I hated pretending to be sick when you called me last week."

"I don't think this day could get any better," Shelby said, looking over at Reed.

"It's only going to get better from here, I promise," he said, pulling her into a tight hug.

The four of them spent the rest of the evening talking, laughing, and catching up. Shelby couldn't stop looking at her mother in disbelief. She'd never been able to visit her new home, and it felt like the best gift she could ever ask for.

Since Gertie had gone to stay next door with Willadeene, Shelby settled her mother and Leanne into the two guest bedrooms upstairs. Afterward, she walked back down to tell Reed goodnight. He wrapped his arms around her, pulling her close.

"This is going to be the best time of our lives," he said.

She looked up at him. "I really believe that's true, and I can't wait."

CHAPTER 13

THE EVENING at Reed's restaurant, Graystone, was nothing short of magical. The rustic charm of the place, combined with the twinkling fairy lights and garlands hanging all over the place, made it like a cozy winter wonderland right in the middle of Charleston. It was what Shelby had always dreamed of: a winter wedding. She wouldn't get that, but at least she could have that experience at her rehearsal dinner.

The whole atmosphere was filled with warmth and joy. There was laughter bouncing around the room. Shelby could hardly believe that in just another twenty-four hours or so, she would be standing at the altar marrying the man of her dreams. As the rehearsal dinner was in full swing, the long wooden tables were filled with people. They were beautifully decorated with candles, greenery, and pops of Christmas red. Reed had made sure that every detail was perfect, right down to the miniature Christmas tree centerpieces and personalized place settings for each of the guests.

Shelby sat at the head of the table right next to Reed, his hand resting on her knee under the table. She just couldn't stop smiling. Her cheeks were hurting so badly that she feared she had sprained them and that maybe her face would stick that way. That's what her mother had always told her as a little kid, and now she worried that she'd be standing at the front of the altar stuck in a permanent smile. There could be worse things, she supposed.

Everything felt so right. The hustle and the stress of the past few weeks were starting to melt away, at least for the evening. The food, as expected, was spectacular. Reed had personally planned the menu with his crew of chefs, and the spread was so indulgent. Perfectly roasted turkey, the most buttery mashed potatoes, grilled vegetables that smelled divine, and all of the holiday trimmings. She dared not to even look at the dessert table. The aroma alone made her stomach rumble and made her fear that she still might not fit into her wedding dress if she wasn't careful.

"This is gorgeous, Reed," Joan said, taking a bite of the turkey. "You've really outdone yourself tonight."

He smiled modestly, as he always did, his arm now draped casually over the back of Shelby's chair.

"Well, I wanted to make sure things were perfect for my future wife here."

"And you've done just that," Joan said with a grin. "I'm not sure how I'll survive without Graystone once I move. No more gourmet dinners on a Tuesday night."

"I'll send you some of my secret recipes," Reed said with a wink. "You'll be making your own restaurant-worthy meals in no time."

She chuckled in response. "Let's be honest. No one can replicate your magic in the kitchen."

The table erupted in agreement, and Shelby's heart swelled with pride for this man that she was about to marry. Not only was he an incredible chef, but he had the most kind and generous spirit. She looked over at him, catching his eye. He smiled at her and made her heart lurch in her chest.

Dinner continued with lively chatter and the clinking of glasses. Lacy was sitting across from

Shelby and leaned across the table. "So Shelby, tell us, are you ready for the big day, or are you still freaking out a little bit?"

Shelby laughed. "Honestly, a little bit of both. I'm excited, but I keep feeling like something else will go wrong."

"Well, that's totally normal," she said, waving her hand dismissively. "Everybody has wedding jitters, but everything will be wonderful, you'll see."

Cami was seated next to Lacy. "And if anything goes wrong, we'll handle it. That's what we're here for. We've got your back."

"Exactly," Joan added. "We've got your back," she repeated.

Shelby smiled at her friends, grateful for their unwavering support. "I don't know what I would do without you guys."

"Totally crash and burn," Lacy teased. "But seriously, don't worry. Reed and I have been working behind the scenes to ensure everything is in place. Nothing is going to fall apart."

Shelby squeezed Reed's knee under the table. "You've been amazing," she whispered to him. "I couldn't ask for a better partner."

"Same goes for you," he said, leaning in and kissing her cheek.

As the evening wore on and the laughter and stories continued, the sense of community and love around the table was palpable, making Shelby feel even more secure in the life she was about to begin with Reed.

After dinner, Reed stood up and tapped his wine glass with a fork, calling the room to attention. "Everyone, can I have your attention for just a minute," he said, his voice commanding the room effortlessly. "I just want to take a minute to thank everybody for being here tonight and for being such a wonderfully important part of our lives. We could not have gotten to this point without your support, and we love each and every one of you."

Shelby's eyes started to well with tears as she listened to him speak. He was always so sincere and so thoughtful, and she couldn't help but feel overwhelmed by finding a man like this to spend her life with.

"I also want to say how incredibly lucky I am to be marrying Shelby," he continued. "You are the love of my life, and I cannot wait to spend forever with you," he said, locking eyes with her. "You've made me a better man, and I'm so grateful that I get to be your husband."

She blushed, with her heart pounding in her

chest. She wasn't sure how she got so lucky, but she was incredibly thankful.

"And," Reed added, glancing around the room, "I'm so grateful that you're all here to celebrate with us. I could not ask for a better group of people to share our lives with."

The room broke into applause, and Shelby hugged him tightly. "I love you," she whispered in his ear.

"I love you more," he whispered back.

When the applause died down, Lacy stood and cleared her throat dramatically. "Well, since Reed gave such a heartfelt speech, I think it's only right that I have a few words as well."

The room fell silent, all eyes turning to Lacy, which was no surprise. She was a beautiful woman, and people typically looked at her anyway.

"I've known Shelby for a while now, and let me tell you, this woman is a force to be reckoned with," she said. "She's strong, funny, smart, and let's be real, she can give as good as she gets. But what I've admired most about her is her ability to love fiercely. When she met Reed, it was obvious that something clicked."

Shelby's cheeks flushed as she listened to her best friend's words.

"Reed, you're a lucky guy. You're marrying one of the most incredible women I know, and I have no doubt that the two of you will build such an amazing life and family together. So here's to Shelby and Reed, to love, to laughter, and to a lifetime of happiness."

Joan raised her glass, toasting the couple as Lacy sat back down.

"Thank you, Lacy," Shelby said.

Reed raised his glass, smiling at Shelby. "To love and laughter," he echoed.

The rest of the evening flowed seamlessly, with everyone mingling and laughing and sharing stories.

Later in the evening, after the dessert had been served—a decadent chocolate mousse cake courtesy of Reed—Joan walked up to Shelby with a knowing smile on her face.

"You're glowing, sweetie," Joan said, hugging her. "I'm so happy for you."

"Thank you, Joan. I'm so glad you're here."

"I wouldn't have missed it for the world. By the way, I have some news."

Shelby raised an eyebrow. "Oh, what's that?"

Joan grinned. "Well, I don't know if you saw me step out to take a phone call."

"No, I guess I was too focused on everything going on."

"I'm not surprised. You should be focused on this. Well, anyway, I got a phone call from my son."

"Oh, is everything okay?" Shelby asked.

"Yes, it's wonderful. I'm not moving after all!"

"You're not moving?" Shelby said, staring at her with her mouth hanging open.

"No, my son surprised me for Christmas with the news that he got a fantastic job opportunity right here in Charleston, so his family is moving here in a few months. They're going to buy a house close to me!"

Shelby's jaw felt like it was hanging onto the floor. "Are you serious, Joan? That's amazing." She hugged her tightly.

"It is, so I'll still be close by, and I'll get to be part of this next chapter of your life."

"That is the best news ever. I am so happy for you and for all of us."

As the evening ended, Shelby realized that she couldn't have asked for anything more. She had been supported by her family, her mom, her soon-to-be sister-in-law, and all of her friends, who were just like family. She knew a lot of people did not feel so blessed by the people they had around them, but she did, and she wished for everyone in the world to feel it, too.

Shelby stood in front of the mirror in her bedroom, adjusting the soft silk robe she had thrown on after she got out of her shower. Her heart was racing. Today was her wedding day. She had a mixture of excitement and nerves bubbling up under the surface. In a few hours, she would walk down the aisle, straight into Reed's arms, and become his wife under the twinkling lights of the backyard. It was Christmas Eve, and the magic of the season had filled every corner of her house for the last few weeks. This was the culmination of the last year of planning.

As she checked her reflection one last time, the door to her bedroom creaked open, and Lacy poked her head in with a grin. "Are you decent?" she asked, laughing.

"Mostly," Shelby said, tying her robe a little tighter. She turned to face her friends, who were now filling the room. Lacy, Cami, Joan, and Willadeene all entered, each holding something small in their hands. Shelby furrowed her brow, curious what they were up to.

Lacy stepped forward first and placed a small velvet box on the edge of the bed. "We wanted to make sure that you had everything you needed on your special day," she said. "You know the tradition: something old, something new, something borrowed, and something blue."

Shelby's heart warmed at the gesture. She had never even thought about her friends doing something like this, but they had been her rock through everything. So why should she be surprised? They had made moving to Charleston easy, made getting over divorce simple, and now made her wedding perfect. She hadn't given much thought to these traditional tokens on her wedding day, but it meant the world to her that they had thought about it.

"I'll go first," Willadeene said, stepping forward with a small, delicate brooch in her hand. It was silver with intricate design and was clearly some kind of family heirloom. "This is something old. My mother wore it on her wedding day, and so did I. I figured it was time for it to be worn by someone else."

Carefully, Shelby took the brooch, feeling its

weight in her hand. "Willadeene, this is absolutely beautiful. Thank you so much."

She huffed a bit and crossed her arms. "Now, don't make a fuss about it," she muttered, though Shelby could see her eyes welling with tears as she turned back and walked to the other side of the room. "And I'll be wanting that back afterward." Shelby couldn't help but chuckle.

"I promise I'll give it right back."

"Willadeene, you didn't have something borrowed. You had something old. You're not supposed to take it back," Lacy whispered loudly.

"It's perfectly fine," Shelby said, winking. "Thank you again, Willadeene."

Joan was next, stepping forward and holding a small satin-wrapped package. "This is something new," she said, handing it to Shelby. Inside was a beautifully embroidered handkerchief with Shelby and Reed's initials tied together with a tiny Christmas wreath. "I had it made for you. A new start, a new family, a new life," Joan said with a smile.

Shelby's eyes filled with tears as she ran her fingers over the delicate fabric. "It's so perfect, Joan. Thank you."

Cami stepped forward with a grin. She held up a pale blue ribbon embroidered with tiny silver snowflakes. "And here's something blue," she said. "I thought it'd be a cute little winter touch for your bouquet."

Shelby smiled, took the ribbon, and held it up. "I love it. It's perfect. Thank you, Cami."

Finally, it was Lacy's turn. She held up a pair of sparkling earrings. "And here's something borrowed," she said. "These were my mom's. She wore them on her wedding day and always said that a bit of borrowed love is the best kind."

Shelby held them in her hand and admired their simple elegance. "Thank you. I don't know what to say. You all have made this day even more special."

The women gathered around, each offering a hug. For a moment, Shelby felt the weight of their love more deeply than ever. They had become family, not just friends.

As they helped her set the brooch inside her dress hanging on the wardrobe and tie the blue ribbon around her bouquet, which was sitting nearby, Shelby smiled, knowing that whatever the day held, she would face it surrounded by the people who loved her and meant the most to her.

"Are you ready for this?" Lacy asked.

Shelby glanced at her reflection again. "I have never been more ready for anything in my life."

Shelby stood by the window in her bedroom, looking out at the twinkle lights that lined the trunks of the two live oak trees in her backyard. It wasn't yet the beautiful setup for her wedding, but she could already envision the ceremony happening beneath the Spanish moss, surrounded by all of her friends and family. The quiet of the house felt like the calm before the storm, and she was allowing herself to just breathe in a little bit of peace for a moment.

The door opened behind her, and Shelby turned to see her mother standing there with a warm and knowing smile. The sight of her mother and just knowing that she was there, looking so vibrant and healthy—or healthier than she had in years—made Shelby feel so grateful. Despite the fact that she had an autoimmune disease, she had made the trip from Tennessee to be with her daughter on her wedding day, and it was a moment Shelby had feared might not happen.

"Hey, sweetheart," she said softly, walking towards her daughter. "Thought I might steal a few quiet moments with you before the chaos begins."

Shelby opened her arms and embraced her

mother tightly. "I'm so glad you did. I could use a few quiet moments myself."

They sat on the edge of the bed, the delicate lace veil hanging from a nearby chair catching Shelby's eye.

"Are you nervous?" her mother asked.

Shelby nodded a little. "Not about marrying Reed, of course, but about everything coming together like it should. Every bride wants her wedding day to be like she envisioned. I just keep imagining something going wrong, or... I don't know, something unexpected happening."

"Well, that's part of the excitement though, isn't it? No wedding has ever gone exactly to plan. The love you and Reed share, that's the only part that matters."

"You always know how to calm me down, Mom," she said, patting her mother's knee. "I've got to remember that it's not about having the perfect day, but the fact that at the end of it, I will be Mrs. Reed Sullivan. Shelby Sullivan. I'll be married to him."

Her mom squeezed her hand. "Exactly. And he's a good man, Shelby, a very good man. I see the way he looks at you like you're his whole world."

Shelby felt tears sting her eyes. She looked down at their hands intertwined. "You know, I never thought I'd find love again after everything I went through. And now, I realize... I don't think I was ever really in love at all. It never felt like this. Reed is different. He makes me believe in second chances."

"And you certainly deserve that second chance. You've been through so much, and yet here you are, stronger than ever, and I couldn't be prouder of you."

"What do you wish for us, Mama, for me and Reed?"

Mona smiled softly. "I wish you peace, Shelby. I wish you laughter and joy and the kind of love that grows stronger with each passing year, just like those live oak trees out in your yard. But most of all, I wish you that kind of marriage where, no matter what happens, you always come back to each other at the end of the day, stronger than ever."

"That's all I've ever wanted too. And now that it's happening, I'm just trying to hold on to it. Reed makes me feel so safe and loved. It's like he knows all my flaws, but he loves me more because of them."

Her mother reached up and tucked a loose strand of hair behind her ear, just as she had done a million times when Shelby was a child. "And that's real love. It's not about perfection; it's about choosing each other every day, even on the hard days."

They sat in silence for a moment, and Shelby felt

a deep sense of peace just to be in her mother's presence. This was the woman who had always been her anchor, and knowing that she was here, feeling better, made her feel like life was more manageable.

Her mom smiled as she looked at Shelby. "You're going to be a beautiful bride, and I want you to know that no matter what life throws at you, you're ready. You have everything you need to be happy."

Shelby leaned in and hugged her mother tightly. "Thanks, Mom. For everything. For always believing in me, even when I didn't believe in myself."

Mona rubbed her back gently. "It's easy to believe in you, Shelby. You've always had the biggest heart, and now you're going to build a family with a wonderful man."

They pulled apart, Shelby feeling the tears rolling down her cheeks.

"I love you, Mama," Shelby said.

"I love you too, sweetheart. Now, let's get you married."

CHAPTER 14

SHELBY WAS GETTING MORE and more nervous as her wedding time approached. She couldn't believe she would be standing at the altar within the hour. She stood in front of her vanity mirror again, adjusting her earrings for what felt like the hundredth time. The anticipation was bubbling up inside of her. That strange sense of unease had settled in, though. Something felt not quite right, but she just couldn't place it.

She looked down at the lace gown that hung beside her, waiting for the perfect moment to slip into it. She wanted to put it on at the very last minute because, with her luck, she would get something on the white fabric right before walking down the aisle. The guests would arrive soon, and the backyard was decorated for the wedding.

But then, the door to the room creaked open, and Lacy stood with an unusually tense look on her face.

"Hey," Lacy said. She had a slightly panicked expression.

Shelby raised an eyebrow. "What's going on?"

Lacy bit her lip, walking in and closing the door behind her. "Okay, Shelby, please don't freak out, but we can't find the rings."

Shelby blinked slowly as she stared at her friend. "The wedding rings? What do you mean you can't find the rings?"

"Well, we've looked everywhere for the box," Lacy said, her voice hushed. "I had them in the little box that you gave me to hold on to, and when I went to check, they were gone."

Shelby's heart started to race. "Gone? Lacy, how can they be gone? They were right here in this house."

"I know," Lacy said, throwing up her hands. "I've been tearing through everything in all the rooms. Joan and Leanne have been helping me, but they're nowhere to be found."

Shelby found herself sinking onto the edge of the bed, her fingers gripping the edge of the mattress.

"Oh my gosh, I don't—I don't know. We can't lose the rings. What are we going to do?"

Lacy sat beside her and wrapped her arm around her shoulders. "Hey, it's going to be fine. We're going to find them. I've got people looking right now."

Shelby shook her head, feeling tears welling up in her eyes. "This can't be happening right now. We're like an hour away from the wedding. Why does it feel like everything is going wrong? Do you think I shouldn't get married?"

Lacy rubbed her back. "Of course, I don't think that. You and Reed adore each other, and you're meant to be together. We've just had a little bad luck with the wedding."

"A little bad luck? First, my venue gets damaged, then my dress doesn't fit, and now you're telling me my rings are missing?"

Lacy looked at her. "Okay, we just need to think logically. Did anybody else have access to this room? Anyone who might have seen the box?"

"I don't know. I mean, the usual people you've seen coming and going, but..." And then a thought hit her. "Wait, Willadeene was in here earlier. She came in again when I was getting ready."

Lacy's eyes narrowed, and she sat up straight. "Are you sure?"

"Of course," Shelby said. "She was in here when you did the little presentation, but then she came back just to check on me, just for a second. I mean, I don't think she would have taken them, do you?"

Lacy's face softened with realization. "Shelby, I think she might have. Not to steal them, but maybe she thought they were a gift for her."

Shelby's eyes widened. "You really think she would have thought that?"

"I mean, it's possible," Lacy said, standing up. "You know how Willadeene is. She's been feeling a little left out lately and a little stressed. Maybe she saw the box and thought she was supposed to keep them safe or something."

Shelby quickly stood. "We have to find her."

Without wasting another moment, the two of them hurried downstairs, Shelby wearing just her slip, and they started weaving through the commotion in the house. Guests were arriving outside, and the bustle of caterers was in full swing in the kitchen. They found Willadeene in the living room, sitting on the couch with her usual grumpy expression. Her arms were crossed over her chest. Shelby had no idea where Gertie was.

"Willadeene," Shelby said, trying to keep her

voice calm but urgent. "We need to talk to you about something."

She looked up. "What is it now? Everything's always a crisis with you young folks."

Lacy stepped forward, trying to keep her voice gentle. "Willadeene, did you happen to see a small box with rings earlier? Maybe you thought it was something for you?"

Willadeene's expression changed slightly, guilt flickering across her face. "I saw a blue box, yes. I thought it was some kind of little wedding gift or something, so I took it. What's the big deal?"

Shelby's heart jumped. "Willadeene, those are my wedding rings. We've been tearing the house apart looking for them."

Her eyes widened. "Oh, those were the rings? I didn't even open it." She reached into her handbag, pulling out the small box. "Why didn't you label it or something? I thought maybe it was for me."

Lacy stifled a laugh. "Why would you think it was for you?"

"I don't know. Maybe I was tired or something," Willadeene said, shrugging her shoulders. Shelby would never understand how that woman thought.

"Well, thank you. We were so worried," Lacy said.

Willadeene waved a dismissive hand. "Well, don't make it such a mystery next time. How was I supposed to know?"

Shelby wanted to ask her why she would take random boxes and assume they were for her without even looking inside, but she had a wedding to prepare for. She didn't have time to have a crazy conversation with Willadeene.

"Well, thank you for keeping them safe," Shelby said.

Willadeene turned her attention to the caterers and crossed her arms again. "Yeah, yeah, just don't go losing anything else."

Shelby and Lacy exchanged a look, both of them trying not to laugh before running back upstairs.

Shelby stood in her kitchen, surrounded by catered food, and looked out the window at the backyard, where she was soon going to walk down the aisle. The soft glow of the twinkling lights wrapped around the live oak trees created a magical space, and the Spanish moss hung elegantly from the branches, swaying gently in the evening breeze. Her heart was pounding, but not from nerves, just the overwhelming flood of emotions that were coming through her all at once.

Her mother, Mona, sat at the table nearby, adjusting the edge of her shawl. Shelby looked down at the lace of her wedding gown, her fingers smoothing the fabric. She loved this dress, and a part of her hoped that one day she'd have a daughter who would wear it and love it too. She knew that was unlikely since wedding dresses went out of fashion pretty quickly. It was much more likely that her daughter would look at it when she was a teenager and scrunch her nose, laughing at her mother's choice.

Taking a deep breath, she turned to her mom, eyes welling with tears. "I'm so glad you're here," she said.

Mona stood up and walked toward her, smiling. "I wouldn't miss this for the world, sweetie. Even if I didn't feel well, I would have had them wheel me in here or put me in a wheelbarrow and just cart me down the aisle."

Shelby chuckled. "That would have been quite a sight."

Mona smiled. "Yes, it would. You know, you've always been my strong, beautiful girl, and today, well, today, you're becoming a wife, and I'm so proud of you."

"I didn't think this day would ever come after my divorce. I was happy to have a new beginning, but I definitely never thought that I would find a love like this. I guess everything happens for a reason."

Her mom reached out and clasped her hand. "Well, you did find it. Reed is an incredible man. He loves you more than anything, and that's all I've ever wanted for you. Someone who sees you and loves you for the wonderful person you are."

"You've always been my biggest supporter. Even when I didn't think I could get through things, there you were, reminding me I was stronger than I thought."

Mona put her hand on her daughter's cheek. "I wish your dad could be here to walk you down the aisle, but I'm very honored that I get to do it, and I know he's watching over you today."

Shelby nodded. "I know he is, and you being here with me, that's everything."

They could hear the distant chatter in the back-yard filtering through the windows, and then the music began to play, signaling that the moment was near.

"I guess it's time," Shelby whispered.

Mona reached for her arm. "Are you ready, my love?"

Shelby took a deep breath and nodded, "More than ready."

Together, arm in arm, they walked toward the back door and stepped outside. The sight before her took her breath away. The yard had been transformed into the most ethereal romantic scene she'd ever seen, even more beautiful than she imagined. In fact, she loved this way more than the church because now, every time she looked down into her backyard, she could remember this beautiful moment.

Soft twinkle lights led her down the path toward the altar. The two oak trees stood tall and majestic, and the moss added to the magical feeling of the moment. Around the base of the trees, Lacy had set up some small lanterns with flickering candles, and they created a pathway toward Reed. Her breath hitched in her throat when she saw him.

He stood at the end of the aisle, his hands clasped in front of him, and his eyes locked on her. The smile on his face was bigger than she'd ever seen, and she was pretty sure he was already crying. He looked more handsome than he ever had, dressed in a tailored suit that made him look like a supermodel.

She could see his eyes welling with emotion, something so raw and powerful that she'd never seen in any other man's eyes when they looked at her. He looked at her like she was the only person in the world.

She looked side to side as she walked down the aisle, noticing the beaming faces of Lacy, Joan, and Cami, who were sitting together, and then she saw Willadeene and Gertie also sitting together on the other side of the aisle. Her heart warmed at the sight of those two sisters who were trying to reconcile, but then her attention was taken right back to Reed, her heart literally skipping a beat when their eyes locked again. She was walking toward her future, that future she couldn't wait to begin.

As she reached the end of the aisle, Reed stepped forward. Mona placed Shelby's hand in his before kissing her daughter on the cheek and taking her seat.

The pastor cleared his throat and began the ceremony. "Dearly beloved, we are gathered here today to witness the union of Shelby Anderson and Reed Sullivan in holy matrimony. This is a day of happiness, love, and commitment as these two people come together to begin their journey as one."

Shelby barely heard the rest of his words over

her pounding heartbeat. She felt like she was floating, like her whole world was centered around this man standing in front of her. She finally understood what people meant when they said they had tunnel vision.

The vows came next. Reed began to speak, his voice steady but filled with emotion.

"I, Reed, take you, Shelby, to be my wife, my partner in life, and my one true love. I promise to cherish you, to laugh with you, to cry with you, to be there for you, and to walk through all of the ups and downs life throws at us for the rest of my life."

Shelby's voice trembled as she recited her own vows. "I, Shelby, take you, Reed, to be my husband. You have been my rock, my constant source of joy and strength, and my soulmate. I promise to love you, to stand by you, to support you, and to build the family that we've always dreamed of."

The rings were exchanged, and they slid them onto each other's fingers. Then, the pastor announced them as husband and wife. Reed turned to Shelby, his eyes sparkling with something she couldn't identify.

"Shelby," he said softly, "I want our life to be full of surprises, and here's my first big surprise as your husband."

Before Shelby could react, she heard the soft hum of a machine, and then suddenly, snow started falling all around them. Real, cold, magical snow drifting down from what seemed like the sky and coating the yard in a blanket of white. Everyone looked up in shock, laughing and squealing as they caught big flakes in their hands.

She gasped, her eyes wide with disbelief. "Reed, how did you—?"

He grinned, pulling her close. "It's Christmas Eve, Shelby, and what's more magical than snow on Christmas Eve?"

As they turned to walk back up the aisle, snow swirling around them, Shelby couldn't stop crying tears of joy. This was more than she had ever dreamed. She looked around at the beauty of the scene, her most perfect winter wonderland wedding, and knew this was exactly how her wedding day was meant to be.

Shelby stood on the makeshift dance floor in her backyard, housed inside a huge tent, snowflakes still softly falling around her, swirling in the air as if they were part of some magical dream. The snow covered the grass in a perfect blanket of white. Even though machines created it, the snow certainly made the backyard feel like a true winter wonderland. It was enchanting and everything she could have imagined, except she never imagined anything this perfect.

The song, *The Way You Look Tonight*, started to play softly in the background, and Reed took her hand, guiding her into his arms for their first dance as husband and wife. She rested her head against his chest, feeling the warmth beneath his suit.

"I still cannot believe you did this," she whispered as they swayed. "A winter wonderland in Charleston. It's like something out of a dream."

Reed smiled at her. "You deserve the best, Shelby, and this is what you wanted. You wanted a winter wedding surrounded by snow, so I did my best to give it to you. I wanted this night to feel magical for you."

She blinked back tears. "It *is* magical. It's more than I could have hoped for, and this certainly couldn't have happened in the church. I can't believe you pulled all this off without me knowing."

He pressed a kiss to her temple. "It wasn't easy keeping this a secret, but seeing that look on your face when that snow started falling made it all worth it."

As they danced, she felt the weight of the past few years and the past few weeks lifting off her shoulders. The heartache from her first marriage, the uncertainty she felt when moving and starting over—all of that seemed so far away now. It was like all of the puzzle pieces suddenly clicked into place. She felt like the luckiest woman in the world right now.

"You've made me so happy, Reed," she said. "I never thought I'd get a second chance at love, but trust me, you've given me more than I ever thought possible. I won't waste this chance."

His grip around her tightened as he pulled her closer. "And you've made me the happiest man alive, Shelby. I can't wait to start our life together. This is just the beginning."

The song ended, and they shared a kiss, with everyone clapping around them as they pulled apart. She felt a wave of gratitude wash over her. Hand in hand, they walked over to talk to their friends. Joan, Lacy, and Cami were standing in the corner holding glasses of wine.

"Look at you two," Lacy called out as they approached. "That was the most romantic first dance I've ever seen. And the snow, come on."

"You didn't help him with that?" Shelby asked.

"No. Reed did that all by himself."

"I will take credit for this one," Reed grinned. "I had a lot of help with everything else, though."

"I don't think I've ever seen anything more beautiful. This night is just perfect," Joan said.

"Thank you to all of you," Shelby said. "You've made this evening more special than I ever could have imagined."

"Well, I would like to propose a toast," Cami said, raising her glass of wine. "To Shelby and Reed for their beautiful wedding and even more beautiful life. And to Joan for getting to stay here on Waverly Lane with us because I can't imagine this place without you. And to me for opening a yoga studio. And to Lacy for all of her career success. I think we're doing pretty dang good," she said, clinking their glasses together.

Before they could say anything else, Willadeene shuffled over and stood there with her hands on her hips.

"And what about me? What about me and my sister talking to each other again?"

Joan chuckled. "That's right, Cami, we can't leave out Willadeene and Gertie."

They held up their glasses again.

"And to Willadeene and Gertie, sisters forever."

"And best friends, too," Shelby added with a smile.

Willadeene grunted. "Well, I don't know about all of that."

CHAPTER 15

SHELBY WOKE up on Christmas morning with a warmth in her heart she'd never felt before. She turned her head on the pillow to find Reed already awake, watching her with that loving gaze that made her feel so safe and cherished.

"Merry Christmas, Mrs. Sullivan," he whispered, kissing her forehead.

She smiled, the sound of her new last name still making her heart skip a beat. "Merry Christmas, Mr. Sullivan."

They lay there for a few moments, wrapped up in each other, in the quietness of the morning. The house was silent except for the faint hum of the heating system.

"How does it feel?" Reed asked, his hand brushing

stray hair away from her face.

"What?" she asked, "being married on Christmas morning? It feels perfect."

He grinned and kissed her quickly before he pulled back the covers and climbed out of bed.

"Well, Mrs. Sullivan, I think it's time we officially celebrate our first Christmas together as a married couple."

She followed him, slipping into her robe, as they made their way downstairs. The smell of the pine candle she had sitting on the living room table filled the air as they passed by the Christmas tree. Reed quickly knelt and plugged it in. Shelby couldn't stop smiling as she glanced around the room, seeing the stockings hanging by the fireplace and the presents waiting under the tree.

Reed walked into the kitchen to start the coffee. After it was finished, he looked back at her as he poured it into the mugs, smiling as if he had something on his mind.

"I do have a surprise for you," he said, setting the mugs on the counter.

She raised an eyebrow, intrigued. "Another surprise? After all the magic you pulled off at the wedding?"

He laughed and walked over to the Christmas

tree, reaching underneath it for a small, beautifully wrapped box. She took the box and unwrapped it. Inside, nestled among the tissue paper, was a brochure. She pulled it out and unfolded it slowly, her breath catching in her throat.

It was an adoption agency brochure. She looked up at Reed, tears welling in her eyes.

"Reed," she whispered.

He stepped closer, taking her hands in his. "I know how much you've always wanted a child, Shelby, and I want to do this with you. I want to build this family together in whatever way feels right for us. You've given me so much love, and I cannot imagine how much love you would be able to give to a child who needs it. I don't want to wait another minute to start our family."

She couldn't hold back tears as they slipped down her cheeks. "You don't know how much this means to me."

He leaned in and pressed a long kiss to her lips. "I think I do."

They stood there for a moment, holding each other, and Shelby thought about this beautiful step toward a future she'd always dreamed of. This was the start of something incredible.

After a few moments, he pulled back. "But that's not the only surprise."

She laughed through her tears. "Wait, there's more?"

He nodded and motioned toward the fireplace. "Grab your stocking."

She wiped her eyes and walked over to the fireplace, pulling down her stocking. Inside, there was another small, wrapped gift. She pulled it out and unwrapped it quickly, revealing a pair of plane tickets to Italy.

"Reed!"

He grinned, stepping up behind her and wrapping his arms around her waist. "Our honeymoon, Mrs. Sullivan. We leave on New Year's Day."

"You really went all out, didn't you?"

"I wanted this Christmas to be unforgettable for both of us. And I plan to top it every Christmas from now on."

She rose up on her tiptoes to kiss him. "You've made it perfect, Reed. Absolutely perfect."

A few moments later, Leanne and Mona joined them downstairs for coffee. They spent the morning opening gifts and enjoying these beautiful moments together as a family. Later, when Leanne and Mona went upstairs, they sat together, curled up on the couch. Shelby couldn't help but think about all of the Christmases to come. Their future together and the family they would build. This Christmas, their first one as husband and wife, was just the start of a life-time of treasures and memories.

EPILOGUE

Six months later

The warmth of early summer filled the air as Shelby sat on the porch swing, rocking back and forth. The yard was in full bloom, vibrant flowers swaying in the soft breeze. She could hear some neighborhood children laughing in the distance. She looked down at the latest issue of *Charleston Wellness Magazine*, where Cami's yoga studio, *Twisted*, was featured in a beautiful spread. The headline read *Charleston's Top Three Yoga Studios You Must Visit*. Shelby felt so proud of her friend. Cami had worked really hard to build something special, and now she had been recognized by a magazine. It made Shelby so excited for her.

"This is amazing," Reed said, walking out onto the

porch with two iced teas. "Cami did such a great job with that studio."

"She really did." Shelby took one of the glasses. "I can't wait to show her this article later. I don't think she's seen it yet."

Reed sat down beside her. "You're a great friend, Shelby Sullivan. And you're an even better wife. I can't wait to see motherhood on you."

Shelby's heart fluttered at the thought. In just a few short weeks, they were becoming parents. A birth mother had chosen them two months ago, and it had been such an emotional rollercoaster ever since. The anticipation of holding their child for the first time filled Shelby with joy and nervousness.

"I still can't believe we're going to be parents soon. I hope I'm a good mom."

"You're going to be a fantastic mom," Reed said.

"I'm going to give it my best shot, that's for sure. I'm *so* ready for this."

He took her hand, squeezing it gently. "*We're* ready for this. I can't wait to meet our little one."

She smiled, leaning her head against his shoulder. They had spent the last few weeks preparing everything—from the nursery to reading every parenting book they could find. The journey of adoption had been an emotional one, but it was all coming together.

Just as Shelby was about to speak, the door swung open. Lacy came bounding onto the porch, waving her phone in the air.

"You guys aren't going to believe this!" she said. She had been there all afternoon, trying to finish some work while her babysitter kept the kids at the house. Shelby had offered her office for a few hours so that Lacy could finish writing. "They've already started casting for the movie adaptation of *Southern Flames*. The studio just called. They've narrowed it down to three actresses for the lead," Lacy said.

"That's incredible!" Shelby said, standing up to hug her. "You must be over the moon with excitement."

"I am," Lacy said, laughing. "It's still so surreal, but it's happening. They're going to start filming by the end of next year."

"Looks like we've got a celebrity in our mix," Reed laughed.

Lacy waved him off. "Hardly, but I'm not complaining. I can't wait to see my name up there on the big screen."

They sat back down to chat, with Lacy joining them in a chair nearby. Then they heard Joan's voice echoing from the sidewalk as she walked up the stairs carrying a basket of fresh vegetables from the farmer's market. Her life had also changed a lot since her son and his family moved to Charleston. She seemed more vibrant than ever. The decision to stay in her home had been the right one. Now, she had the best of both worlds. She got to live near her son and his family while staying on Waverly Lane. She was still dating Randy, and they were talking about marriage.

"Well, you're just in time," Shelby called out to Joan. "Lacy's movie is really happening."

"Of course it is," Joan said, smiling as she climbed the porch steps. "And I expect front-row seats when you have the premiere. I hope it's someplace fancy. Can we do it in Paris?"

The group laughed as Joan set the basket down before joining them on the porch.

As the conversation flowed, Shelby's thoughts turned to Willadeene. She and Gertie had made so much progress over the last few months. Gertie officially moved in with her. And though their relationship was still rocky at times—primarily because of Willadeene's perpetual bad mood—there were more good days than bad. Shelby had found herself acting as a mediator whenever an argument came up. But

Willadeene had softened a bit, admitting that she appreciated having her sister around as they grew older. Gertie had even joined the book club, much to everyone's surprise. She wasn't as vocal as Willadeene, but she did find her place in the little group.

The two sisters had even vacationed with some of Gertie's lottery winnings. They'd visited Scotland, where their family originally came from, which surprised the heck out of Shelby. She worried the two of them would kill each other before they made it back home.

"How's Willadeene?" Lacy asked as if reading Shelby's mind.

"I think she and Gertie are doing okay. You know, it's not always smooth sailing, but they seem to have realized how much they missed each other all these years."

"That's all that matters," Joan said, smiling knowingly. "Sometimes it takes time to mend fences within a family, but at least they're together now."

Despite the ups and downs, there was so much to be grateful for. Shelby's friends were thriving, her community was strong, and soon, she and Reed would welcome a child into their lives. Her mother had even toyed with the idea of moving in with them just to be closer. Shelby hoped that she would do that so that their child would have a grandmother right there in the house.

As the sun set over Waverly Lane, casting its usual beautiful golden glow over the neighborhood, Shelby knew this was just the beginning of a beautiful new chapter for each of them. They had come through so much together, and now, as her found family, they were all ready to support each other through whatever the future held.

Want more Rachel Hanna books? Visit store. RachelHannaAuthor.com and click on Reading List.

Made in the USA
Las Vegas, NV
01 December 2024

13071858R10146